SCARLETT IN KNOWARE

To Frankie

SCARLETT IN KNOWARE

STUART FRYD

GE

Greenwich Exchange
London

Greenwich Exchange, London

First published in Great Britain in 2020
All rights reserved

Scarlett in Knoware © Stuart Fryd 2020

Printed and bound by imprintdigital.com
Cover design: December Publications
Tel: 07951511275

Greenwich Exchange Website: www.greenex.co.uk

Cataloguing in Publication Data is available from the British Library

ISBN: 978-1-910996-36-2

To Gran, thank you

1

The Journey to Knoware

IT WOULD HAVE BEEN A BEAUTIFUL sight from the station platform – the last of the daylight had drained away, leaving a crimson streak across the horizon. Soft pinks and purples crowned the darkening rural landscape and flecked everything with a rosy, golden light. Bare trees were silhouetted against the soft hues of the on-coming night, swallows swooped and darted, the platform hanging baskets cascaded with violets – but Scarlett was busy staring at her phone, so she saw none of these things. She whistled away to herself in her G-Star blue jeans, red Converse trainers and her favourite red puffer jacket, the hood of which was pulled up, hiding her long, dark hair.

Why did she have to go to her dad's this weekend? All her friends looked like they were already having such a good time. Her iPhone pinged and peeped and shook as messages from various apps popped up, reminding her of what a good time she was missing. Her thumbs scrolled and swiped and typed; her face illuminated by the harsh, blue glow of the screen in the fading daylight. Photos of all of them in Lily's bedroom laughing and dancing and not looking like they were missing her in the slightest filled her notifications. She watched a video of them all singing, and chuckled, but her laugh stuttered and got stuck in her throat as a tinge of jealousy rose up within her. Seeing her dad was great ... at least it had been at first.

Since her parents had split up, her dad had moved out to the next village along. Now, if the small town where she currently lived with her mum was remote, then her dad's village of Mournt may as well have been in the middle of Siberia. In fact, she was quite sure there were isolated villages in the middle of the Amazon rainforest that had more to do on a Saturday night than Mournt did. You had to climb to the roof to get a mobile phone signal and not a soul in the village, apart from her dad, had ever even heard of broadband. Mournt had one tiny shop that never seemed to be open and besides, she was banned from going in it now because of the whole misunderstanding about how she forgot to pay for the chewing gum that ended up in her pocket.

Travelling to Mournt to see her dad always felt like she was travelling back in time, as if the world got slower and greyer the closer to Mournt she got. As much as she hated to admit it, traveling to her dad's just made her feel she was missing out on everything. Poppy's fifteenth birthday – missed it. Bonfire night at school – missed it. Lily's sleepover – missing it.

Why couldn't her dad have found a flat the other side of town, or at least moved to the city? Somewhere a bit closer to life, to people, to music. But her dad had told her he was a country boy at heart. He had met Scarlett's mother when they were both students in their twenties. There were plenty of photos proving her mum and dad had loved each other once, but none of these photos were on the mantelpiece or windowsills anymore. Their love only existed in boxes on the top of her mum's wardrobe now. That left Scarlett travelling between the two of them and wondering when her life would begin.

Ambling along towards her, lit up by the track's floodlights, came her train. The only train. She guessed by its distance it would still be another eight or so minutes until it arrived. This was always the train's final journey of the week and it seemed to know it. It barely got above a walking pace as it trundled from the city, through the towns and villages to the last two stops on the line; her mum's sleepy town and the edge of the known world, the middle of nowhere, the village that time forgot – Mournt.

Her dad would already be waiting for her there probably, dressed in his ripped jeans with his brown suede jacket, grinning as her train pulled in. The best part of his week, he would say, but she was having to miss out on another party.

Scarlett sent replies to all her messages and opened all the photos and videos she could as they came pouring in, knowing that her signal would cut out virtually as soon as the train left the station. Suddenly a photo popped up of Daisy. Daisy was there. She'd been in Dubai for the last year and now was back. Everyone was getting to see her and catch up and she would have to wait until Monday. The evening was just getting worse and any second now she would have to get on the train and sever her umbilical cord to the real world for the next two days.

Reluctantly, the old train dragged itself alongside the platform and sighed and sagged as it stopped. It was a single carriage vehicle that looked as though it was the uncared-for baby of a Victorian steam train and a fairground ride. It was made from iron, painted a dull burgundy with wooden panels of walnut. It must have been the only train in the country that still had handles on the doors you had to open yourself. Brass handles! And good luck to you if you had a bike or a backpack or were pregnant because the single door to get on wasn't wide enough for modern humans. Perhaps when it was designed in the dark ages for people whose average size was four-foot-tall it was fine, but trying to get in with an overnight bag, even one as modestly sized as hers, meant getting on sideways. After chucking her backpack into the carriage, she squeezed in after it, trying not to scuff or tear her red puffer jacket as she got on.

Fortunately for her there was never anyone in the carriage for this final stretch before the train could collapse and rest for the night. The whole carriage was hers – Queen of dated and dusty upholstery. She could sing and dance and do acrobatics the whole way if she wanted to. She didn't. Instead, she took a photo of herself looking suitably sad among the empty orange and brown leather chairs titled: ENJOY YOUR NIGHT GIRLS! I WISH I NEVER HAD TO GO TO MY DAD'S!

Scraping over the tracks, the train began to drag itself out of the station like a reluctant donkey on its last legs and her phone-signal bar dropped to zero and flashed a NO SERVICE sign. Madly, she tried to mash the send button, but a message popped up saying her photo had failed to deliver. That was it, contact lost. She'd hear nothing of the party now until Sunday night.

Putting her phone in her pocket with a sigh, she pressed her forehead against the glass and stared out of the window whistling Jonas Blue's 'Rise' to herself. It seemed fitting. She'd always been told she had a good whistle.

Fields, illuminated now only by twilight, bounced slowly by and were replaced with woodland. Unlike on any previous occasion she had travelled to her dad's though, the train began to slow with a terrible whine of metal against metal. The old train could hardly have been travelling much more than a jogging pace, but it still seemed to take an age to grind to a halt.

Scarlett peered out the window to try to see what the matter was. Ahead of them was a red signal light burning out of the darkness. It was then that she saw, for the first time, that the railway track broke off into a separate line here. A branch of track separated from the one they were on and stretched off into the distance. It would have been impossible to see the other track in the dark had it not been illuminated by white overhead lights. Why had she never noticed this track before?

This was all very odd. Why was the light red? There was only one track and only one train, so it wasn't waiting for another train to pass. And where did this other track branch off to? There were no other stops on the map. There wasn't even another village or farmhouse between her mum's town and Mournt. She got her phone out to google where it went, then put it back in her pocket with a huff as she remembered she had no signal. Where did that line go?

It couldn't have been for another train, as there weren't any others. Maybe there was a repair shed or something further along?

But it seemed strange to waste all that electricity to light up a bit of track that was never used.

The wait at the red light continued to drag on. Yawning, she stretched out and put her feet up on the seat opposite. There was no one around to give her dirty looks, after all. Puffs of dust lazily swirled into the air around her trainers. Besides, the week had been a busy one, what with almost getting caught sneaking out to the cinema by her mum the night before, and she felt unusually tired. In fact, she could barely keep her eyes open. Feeling dozy and fuzzy and warm, she tried not to sleep by coming up with a compromise with herself. She would just close one eye and keep the other half open. It worked for almost a minute and, just as she was drifting off again, she imagined she saw, through her half-closed eye, the train begin to move again, heading onto the other set of tracks that stretched off into the woods. Then she was fast asleep.

2

The Bridge

WIPING AWAY THE DRIBBLE FROM HER chin, she stretched and blinked. The train had stopped. It was cold and dark, and the creaky train was silent, as if it had finished its journey some hours ago and it was now fast asleep. Grabbing her bag, she threw the train door open, squeezed out and dropped to the platform. The station was in total darkness. Fear and the cold night air hit her, and she immediately felt awake, her heart thumping.

'Dad?' she called out, the word turning to steam in the chill of the air. 'Dad?' she called again, but this time louder and squeakier as the wait for a reply dragged on.

Why wasn't he there? He was always there, leaning against the lamppost, dressed in his scruffy jeans and suede jacket. That's how it had been every week for the last year. But he wasn't there now. Her bag suddenly felt very heavy, and she let it drop to the floor next to her. Tears began to well in her eyes and she just stood there, looking around her. Where was he? He should be here.

She checked her phone. No signal, of course. Nothing at all, in fact. Her phone was dead. She held the power button down but there wasn't even a flicker of life. But that couldn't be right. She had left home with eighty percent battery. It was impossible to have used up all that power unless – unless it was a lot later than she thought.

Maybe she had been sitting in the train for hours. Maybe her dad had given up and driven off and it was so late that the station had shut and turned off all the lights. But that was silly – her dad would have checked the train and seen her asleep.

Stuffing her useless phone into her pocket, she picked her bag up and decided she had no choice but to walk to her dad's house. Doing anything was better than just standing there in the dark. It wasn't far, and it was a straight enough walk. Scarlett wasn't scared of the dark or being mugged, because almost no one lived in Mournt. It was the kind of village where getting caught for stealing chewing gum from the village shop would make the local paper, but, luckily for her, Mournt was too small for a local paper. Not that the lack of a local paper stopped the whole village finding out about the chewing gum theft. Gossip was rife in the small village with everyone knowing everyone else's business.

Setting off out of the station at a good pace, she passed a few of the old houses and headed up the cobbled lane. From somewhere far off an owl hooted. But apart from this one interruption, the night was silent. The silence grew until it became oppressive, almost claustrophobic, so she started to whistle a Billie Eilish song.

Scarlett thought about knocking at one of the houses and asking for help but all the lights were off, and she didn't want to get people out of bed on her account. It was then that Scarlett noticed the sky.

It was incredible. It was the clearest night she had ever seen. Every single star in the sky, and a million others that had never made themselves known before, shone down with crystal clarity. When her dad had pointed out the Milky Way to her before it had just been a slightly brighter smear of stars than those around it. But now the Milky Way was a proud band of sparkling silver that flowed through the darkness like a river. Scarlett stood there, unable to even whistle as she just stared at the sky open mouthed for ages before she remembered where she was and how she had to find her dad soon. He was bound to be worried and he may have even resorted to phoning her mum and then that would start a fight.

Striding on, she passed a few more cottages with their windows dark and their curtains drawn, until she heard voices. The noise was coming from the village pub. Relief washed over her and she sighed, pleased that there were at least others alive and awake in the world beside herself.

Scarlett knew the pub well. It was called The Faraway Frontier and her dad had often taken her there for Sunday lunch when he couldn't be bothered to cook – which wasn't often, to be fair to him. As she came closer, though, she noticed that the pub must have recently changed its name because the sign that hung from its dark timber frame no longer said The Faraway Frontier. In the starlight she could see it was called The Three Pigs and had a painted sign of three pigs outside a straw house. It didn't look like a new sign, though, and Scarlett thought it strange to change a pub's name and then put up an old sign.

Ignoring the name change, Scarlett walked around to the front of the pub and looked through the tiny, lead-paned windows. The glass was all steamed up and dirty, but she could see the blurry shapes of figures inside. There was evidently a party going on because everyone was wearing fancy dress and dancing or playing darts. There was what looked like a pig, a goose, maybe a couple of people in bear costumes, all dancing around the pool table to a tune a cat was playing on a fiddle. The costumes all looked very realistic, but then it was very hard to see anything clearly through the grime and condensation. She could see that the only light inside came from candles scattered about the room, on tables and on the mantelpiece. Maybe there had been a power cut? Scarlett thought it odd that the usually docile residents of Mournt would be dressed up and out at that late hour, but maybe she had just never looked properly before on the ride over to her dad's house.

Deciding that she would feel embarrassed if she went in and spoiled their party – all accusing eyes on the chewing gum thief – Scarlett carried on up the track. If he wasn't at home she would come back to the pub and ask to use their phone. If the worst came to the worst, Scarlett would call her mum from the pub and her mum would come and pick her up, although she didn't want to get her dad in trouble.

The road she walked up was a single lane track that had been built hundreds of years ago for two horses to just about pass each other, and it didn't look as though it had been repaired much since then. The many potholes that marred her way were more akin to small ponds and Scarlett found herself ankle deep in icy water numerous times before she reached the bridge. She was quite sure she remembered the stone bridge being wider than this, but she guessed she hadn't paid much attention in the car.

When she reached the middle of the bridge, Scarlett heard shuffling in front of her, and she froze. Out of the blackness, from the other end of the bridge, shuffled an old lady. She was dressed in a long, black dress with a black, woollen jacket and a blood-red shawl wrapped tightly around her. Over her hair she wore a purple scarf and she smiled when she looked up and saw Scarlett. It was Scarlett's normal reaction to avoid old ladies in Mournt. They always watched her very closely without ever trying to hide the fact they didn't trust her. It wasn't as if she was going to try and steal anything here again, was it?

'Hello, my darling,' the old woman croaked in a raspy voice as she hobbled nearer. 'You're not from around here, are you?'

'No, I'm not. I'm just heading to my dad's house, but I'm late and he'll be terribly worried,' Scarlett replied, and, now that the old woman was closer, Scarlett could see just how ancient she was. The old woman's leathery, wrinkled skin – framed by the thinnest bone-white hair – looked as though it could blow away like dust in the merest breeze.

'Well, you did wish you didn't have to go to your father's,' the old lady said, and flashed a wicked grin. Scarlett was so shocked that she actually stumbled backwards into the bridge wall and would have fallen over into the river had the old lady not reached out and grabbed her arm, pulling her back with a strength that would have been impressive from a teenage girl. 'Now, be careful, my darling. You must watch where you step', and as she said this she seemed to notice something behind Scarlett. 'Oh darling, you've snagged your pretty red jacket', and, before Scarlett could gasp or turn away, the old lady produced a pair of ornate scissors from her pocket and snipped at the air twice behind Scarlett's back. 'There you go. All better.' The old lady smiled smugly as she stuffed the scissors and something else inside her pocket. 'All done. Good luck finding your father,' she said, her grey withered lips stretching wide to give Scarlett a toothless grin as she turned away, shuffling off into the darkness.

If the old woman had slapped her, Scarlett would have been less shocked. It was the strangeness of the whole incident – and the comment. How had the old lady known what she had typed when she got on the train? What was she doing out here by the bridge in the middle of the night?

Taking a deep breath, Scarlett staggered to the other side of the bridge, her shoes still sloshing with cold water. She clutched her stomach and then felt her head as if she would faint. Something was wrong. Scarlett checked her pockets to see if her phone and purse were still there – they were – but she felt as though she was now missing something – as if she had just been robbed. She tried to picture what the old lady had done. Were the scissors just a distraction so she could take something else? She shook the thought from her head. She was just being silly.

Old ladies didn't go around mugging people in the middle of the night, especially not in Mournt.

To her great relief, after a few more minutes of walking, her dad's house came into view. But her relief was short-lived, and she felt her stomach churn as she saw that all the lights were out. There was no car out the front of the house and it looked like no one was home. Maybe he was driving around looking for her? Walking up to the old farmhouse, she tried to peek into the living-room, but the curtains were tightly shut, which was strange because Scarlett could have sworn her dad had blinds in the living-room. The front door was locked, so she went around the back of the house, being confident it would still be open as most people in Mournt still left their back doors unlocked. Scarlett smiled when the door swung open with the gentlest of pushes. It was pitch black inside the kitchen and after a few moments trying to find the light switch, she gave up and opened the living-room door. This room was in total darkness too and she couldn't find the light switch here either. Had her dad removed the light switches? Her friend Tina's dad had taken all the light switches off the walls in their flat and now you controlled everything with your voice, but Tina's dad had a swanky apartment with lots of tiny cacti and stone Buddhas. Scarlett's dad lived in a converted farmhouse which still smelled like a zoo. In fact, today the animal odour seemed far worse than normal. Her dad was normally pretty good at looking after himself, but the room definitely had a musty, farm smell.

Putting the lack of lighting and the strange smell to the back of her mind, she went upstairs. Had he had the carpet on the stairs taken up? Over the creak of the floorboards, she heard snoring coming from her dad's room and a wave of anger washed over her. Asleep! Her dad was asleep! She was missing in the middle of the night, and he had just gone to bed. Overcome with emotion, Scarlett stormed into the darkness of her room and went to turn the light on, but again, the light switch wasn't there. After feeling her way around the walls, she cried out in frustration, not caring how much noise she made, wanting to wake her dad up.

Hot with anger, she went to collapse on her bed. But it wasn't there either. The bed had been moved closer to the window. How dare he start to change her room around without her consent, she thought as she pulled off her red puffer jacket, scrunching it as small as she could and throwing it into the corner. She kicked off her Converse trainers, hoping to wake her dad up with all the noise so that she could tell him how mad she was, but the snoring continued. Well fine, she thought. She would just ignore him in the morning, and she would call her mum to pick her up and that reminded her to charge her phone. Taking her mobile from her pocket, she dug out a charger from the bottom of her bag, flinging her clothes around the room in frustration. As she plugged her phone into the charger, she felt around the walls for the power socket but to no avail. It was as if the power sockets had all been removed too and, with tears of hurt, anger and frustration rolling down her cheeks, she gave up, dropping her phone and getting into bed.

It took a long while for sleep to come, though. She tossed and turned and took her frustration out on her pillow. It didn't help that her bed now felt all hard and lumpy. Her dad must have swapped her mattress for an old one because she never remembered it being this uncomfortable before. Then the old lady's face flashed in front of her and her frustration turned to an unknown fear. Underlying everything was the feeling that something was missing. It was like that feeling you get when you know you've forgotten something but can't remember what. Despite the storm of emotions, the uncomfortable bed and the fact she had dozed on the train, sleep finally came to her.

3

Scarlett in Knoware

IN THE MOMENTS BEFORE SCARLETT OPENED her eyes the previous night came flooding back to her. It all felt more like a dream than something that had actually happened. Had her dad really just fallen asleep and forgotten to pick her up? She opened her eyes and sat up. That was when she saw the three bears.

Really she should have screamed then. That would have been a perfectly natural and normal response – to scream when you see three, very real looking bears standing at the end of your bed intently watching you. But she stared back at them quite calmly, as her still very sleepy brain tried to work out what was going on. It was probably still a dream, or maybe they were costumes, like the people were wearing in the pub the night before. But if it was a dream, it was a very real dream, and the longer Scarlett stared at them without anything else happening the more real it became. Dreams didn't have awkward pauses, at least, no dream that Scarlett could remember did. And the more she stared at their eyes – their big, round, brown, very-non-human eyes and at their sharp, definitely-bear-like teeth, she realised they *were* bears. Scarlett definitely should have screamed then. She wanted to – her brain had registered that the three giant predators were very real and in her bedroom – but she hadn't screamed yet and they hadn't attacked yet, so maybe she should just stay very still and very quiet.

So the staring went on, with the bears just looking at her, and Scarlett staring right back at them in turn. Then she noticed some odd things. For instance, the largest bear was wearing a chef's hat and an apron and the smallest bear, still a good five-foot-tall on its hind legs as it currently stood, was wearing a red baseball cap.

'Well good morning, Miss,' the bear in the middle said in a sweet voice.

This took a lot of processing and Scarlett could almost hear her brain fizzing in confusion. Scarlett decided that now would be a good time to scream. So she did. It was a good, long, glass-shattering scream that went on until Scarlett turned scarlet and ran out of breath. Then she grabbed the blanket and covered herself up. The logical part of her brain knew that a blanket was a fairly weak defence against bears, but that part of her brain also knew that this was not a logical situation. Bears didn't talk or dress up. And there certainly weren't any bears in Mournt. That would have been far too exciting. So this wasn't happening and, because it wasn't happening, hiding under her blanket was a perfectly reasonable response.

'Don't tell me. The bed was too lumpy, or it was too soft,

right?' the largest bear in the apron said in a gruff tone as it tore
the blanket away from Scarlett, leaving her sitting there, hugging
her knees.

Scarlett went to reply and then her brain stopped her, because
to hear voices coming from animals was one thing, but to start
talking back was quite another.

'Oh don't listen to him, dear. We had a girl about your age
stay a while back. Turned up out of the blue just like you. She
ran off without paying and shouted some terrible things about
our home. The furniture was too small or too large and the food
was too hot or too cold. We haven't had a guest since. But now
you're here,' the middle bear said pleasantly.

'You going to run off without paying?' the big bear said,
looming over the bed.

'Stop it, Daddy Bear. You're scaring our guest,' the middle
bear said, putting a placating paw on the big bear's chest.

'Can I keep her, Pa?' the little bear chimed in.

'We'll see if she pays. If not, you can keep her,' Daddy Bear
replied, and grunted as he lumbered out of the room.

'So, my darling, where are you from?' the middle bear said as
she opened the windows and the warm morning light streamed
in and coated every mote of dust in gold.

Scarlett wanted to believe this was a dream, but all the details
screamed to her that it wasn't. The gingham curtains, every strand
of brown fur on the bears' bodies, the smell of cooked bread
coming from downstairs. This was real.

'Mournt. I was going to Mournt,' Scarlett said, before her
brain could stop her replying to the talking animals.

'I'm not sure I've heard of Mournt. Is it south, near the Giant Bean Stalk? Or west, towards the Magic Forest?'

'I got on the 19:37 train to Mournt,' Scarlett said, shaking her head. Why – how – was she having this conversation?

'Oh,' the medium-sized bear nodded, as if that explained everything. 'You're one of them.'

'Who? One of who? Where am I? How did I get here?' Scarlett said as a thousand questions raced through her mind. The middle-sized bear gave her a puzzled look.

'You just said, you came by train.'

'Yes, I know I came by train, but how did it end up here? Where even is here?'

'Well, darling. The Choo-choo train followed the tracks and the tracks led here,' the bear said, as if she were talking to a three-year-old. 'And here is the Three Bears' Bed-and-Breakfast, where you can always expect a warm meal and a comfy bed,' she reeled off, as if this was a well-worn phrase she used for promotional purposes. 'Despite what some recent reviews may say.'

'And where is your bed-and-breakfast? I mean, what town is this?'

'This is the village of Hapglade, which is in the south of the Land of Knoware and, by the smell of it, breakfast is ready. Get yourself dressed and come and join us,' the middle bear said, brightly.

'So, can I keep her?' the little bear asked, as he was guided out of the room by what was evidently his mother.

'Maybe, darling,' she replied, as they trudged down the stairs.

Scarlett was glad to be alone for the moment. She tried all the things you're supposed to do when faced with a sight that is too amazing or confusing to be believed. She rubbed her eyes, tried blinking hard and even splashed her face with some warm water from a bowl on a little table by the window. Despite all of this, she was still in a strange bedroom.

Where her white Ikea wardrobe should have been was an old oak cupboard. The television that should have been on the wall opposite the bed was a rather crude painting of the three bears, and her white duvet was now a greying blanket. The floorboards were bare but polished timbers, the lamp on her bedside table was a candle stick and the whole place had a fresh pine smell to it. Not just a car air-freshener pine smell, but an actual pine smell.

She went to the open window and took a deep breath to try to calm herself down, but the view did the exact opposite.

From the window, she watched a family of geese, the smallest of which must still have been four-foot-tall, waddle past the house – all of them wearing waistcoats or bonnets. The goose in front had a bundle of books under one wing and she kept honking at the geese behind her to keep up. Opposite, a pig was standing on its hind legs leaning against a shop window dressed in golfing trousers, a flat cap and smoking a pipe. He noticed her at the window and took his pipe out from beneath his snout, raising it in greeting as he gave her a little nod and then took no more notice.

Shutting the window, Scarlett went back to sit on her bed. It really was uncomfortable. Taking a deep breath, she looked around her room that clearly wasn't her room and resigned herself to the fact that she had either gone totally mad and was hallucinating, or she was actually in another world. It was funny to find herself hoping that she had just gone mad.

After freshening up as best she could, she collected the clothes she had thrown about the room the night before and chose something to wear. Pulling on her favourite red jacket, she walked to the top of the stairs. Below, she could hear china cups tinkling on saucers and something sizzling in a pan. It all sounded so normal. But there were bears down there. Bears that could easily eat her if they wanted to. But they hadn't yet, and that gave her hope. Repacking her bag and slinging it over her shoulder, she made her way down the first few steps. The bears were eating their breakfast around a table which was covered in a gingham cloth. The kitchen was low and cool, with wooden cupboards and jolly porcelain human figures covering every space. A chimney sweep and a milkman smiled up at her from the windowsill as Scarlett said good morning, chewing her fingernails as the bears paused to look up at her.

'Well,' Mummy Bear said, pulling out a chair by the breakfast table. 'Don't just stand there, come and eat.'

'And don't chew your fingers, or there'll be none left for Baby Bear. The fingers are his favourite part,' Daddy Bear said, and Scarlett froze, her eyes wide. She looked to the back door, calculating if she could make a dash for it before they got her, but Baby Bear began to roar with laughter, breaking the tension.

'Just ignore Daddy Bear's sense of humour,' Mummy Bear soothed, guiding her to a chair and then pouring her a cup of tea.

'That was funny, Pa,' Baby Bear said, when he had finally stopped laughing.

With a trembling hand, Scarlett moved the porcelain figure of a young girl in a bonnet out of the way and spooned some porridge into her bowl. It smelled divine and Scarlett realised how hungry she was, remembering now that she had missed dinner the night before. She blew on her porridge as the bears watched her with interest. The porridge was delicious, although a little too hot.

'You planning on staying long?' Daddy Bear asked, between great spoonfuls of porridge.

'No, I hadn't planned on staying at all. I'm just going to go back to the station to head home as soon as I can,' Scarlett replied. Daddy Bear began to nod and slowly lowered his spoon back down onto the chequered tablecloth.

'Oh, I see,' he said in a slow, measured voice, his eyes fixed intently on her.

'Don't, Daddy Bear,' Mummy Bear said, putting her paw on his. He pulled it away as if he had been stung.

'No, I get it,' he said, folding his arms, still staring at her. 'You don't like the place. You don't like the effort Mummy Bear put in to make your porridge! You think our chairs are too big, right? Or the sun was too bright through your window.'

'That's not what she meant, dear,' Mummy Bear said, trying to calm him down.

'No, no,' Scarlett protested, moving her chair back from the table instinctively. 'The porridge is lovely.' And to prove it, she spooned another mouthful in. It burnt the inside of her mouth, but she hid it well. 'It's the best bed-and-breakfast I've ever stayed at, actually. The bed was so comfy,' she said, her mouth still half-full of porridge. 'Amazing. Five stars. Really!'

Daddy Bear began to nod slowly. 'Good. Good. And the room? Your room was okay?'

'Much better than okay. The best. So ... so rustic!' Scarlett said, nodding enthusiastically.

'Well, that's fine then,' he said, leaning back, seemingly satisfied.

'You have to understand, dear,' Mummy Bear said, putting her paw on Scarlett's hand, dwarfing it under hers, 'this place is his pride and joy.'

'It really is lovely. I'd love to stay. But I should be getting back now. My dad will be worried.'

'I understand completely. Now, how will you be paying?' Mummy Bear said, popping on a pair of reading glasses and opening a leather-bound book. 'That's one night, full breakfast,' she paused a second, running her claw along the line in her ledger to check their prices. 'One silver tab, please.'

'Oh. Right. The thing is – I don't have any silver tabs,' Scarlett said, rummaging around in her jeans' pockets and putting some loose change on the table. 'I have these.'

Daddy Bear peered at the coins and Mummy Bear nudged them with a claw suspiciously. 'I'm afraid none of these coins are accepted here. What else do you have?'

'She's got fingers, Mum!' Baby Bear said, as he licked his lips and stood up on his stool, leaning closer to get a better look at them.

'No, darling. Not yet, anyway,' Mummy Bear said with a smile. 'Anything else?'

Scarlett tipped out the contents of her bag onto the table. 'I have my phone. It needs charging, but it's – ' she stopped as Daddy Bear tested the phone between his teeth, shattering the screen.

'Nope,' he said, tossing it back onto the table.

'No worries. I have some gloves,' she said, holding up a pair of gloves she had got for Christmas the year before. Baby Bear tried to put his paw in one, but his claws tore right through the material and the glove fell to the table in ribbons. 'Okay, not to worry, I have some perfume. It's Dolce & Gabbana!'

Mummy Bear took the bottle, sniffed it and, before Scarlett could protest, she pulled the lid off and drank it.

'That's revolting!' Mummy Bear said, grabbing her cup of tea and gulping it down to wash the taste away.

'Is that all you have?' Daddy Bear said, standing up. 'How many fingers make up a silver tab?'

'I'm not sure, darling,' said Mummy Bear as she stretched out to reach a drawer in the sideboard and took out a quill and a bottle of ink. Dipping the quill into the ink, she began to scratch some jottings in the back of the ledger. 'Oh look,' she said, reaching for a napkin to dab at the blossoming ink splodge the quill had dripped. 'Silly me. I do so hate it when the ink does that.'

'Wait – wait!' Scarlett said, unzipping the front compartment of her rucksack, throwing her geography book to one side and delving to the bottom to pull out two biros. They were only half-full of ink and the lids had been chewed, but Scarlett saw them as her one shot of getting out of there with her fingers intact. The three bears stared at the pens in her hand.

'Watch!' and she took the ledger from Mummy Bear and began to write. 'PLEASE. DON'T. EAT. MY. FINGERS,' she narrated as she wrote the words out in capital letters. 'No ink spills, no mess.' The bears looked at each other and nodded approvingly. 'In my village, one of these pens would normally cost at least three silver tabs, but I'm willing to give you both pens to show my appreciation of just how lovely my room was.'

'That will do nicely,' Daddy Bear said, and he and Mummy Bear took a pen each to examine closer.

'Well, thank you for everything, and for not eating me, but I really do have to get back now,' Scarlett said, stuffing her possessions back into her bag and walking to the door.

'You come back any time, you hear?' Mummy Bear said, grabbing her as she made for the door, sweeping her off her feet into a bear-hug. It was like being crushed in a giant, furry vice, but Mummy Bear plonked her down again with only minor bruising to Scarlett's ribs. The three bears stood at the door and waved her off as Scarlett walked into the bright morning sunshine.

The path was made of neat flagstones which cut through a beautifully tended garden of manicured grass, red tulip borders and passionflowers climbing the walls in full bloom. Scarlett opened the low gate at the end of the garden and waved back, making her way towards where she thought the direction of the station was. It was time to get back to Mournt, where her dad would be frantically waiting.

'I can do this. I can do this. Just keep walking. Don't talk to
the other animals unless you have to,' she said under her breath
as she tried not to make eye contact with the numerous beasts
that strolled past her quite comfortably on their hind legs. The
whole of the village looked quite different to her father's village
of Mournt in the daylight. There seemed to be far more houses
and buildings here now than there had been the night before.
Or maybe she just hadn't noticed them because she hadn't been
looking for them. The centre of the village was a large cobbled
square with market stalls scattered almost randomly about it.
Surrounding the square on all four sides were lines of old shops.
There were a number of tailors, a candlestick maker, a cake shop,
a baker. All the animals were milling around in old-fashioned
clothes. There was a cat, dressed in a bonnet and maid's outfit
who ignored her totally and various rabbits about her own height
wearing waistcoats and trousers. Scarlett walked out of the square
and headed towards where she hoped the station was – where it
would be in Mournt.

'Hello!' Scarlett heard a squeaky voice calling out to her as
she was putting some distance between herself and the main
square. Scarlett ignored it and kept her head down, walking as
fast as she could. 'I say – Hello! Can you help me?' Scarlett glanced
up and caught the eye of a pig dressed in a sailor's suit which was
made up of a pair of smart, white trousers and a white top which
didn't quite meet. It left a band of pale, pink tummy between
them that Scarlett couldn't help staring at. The pig had topped
the look off with a blue kerchief wrapped around his podgy neck
and a little, round, white hat and he was struggling to lift a bale

of straw above his head. The pig stood in a rough square of
haybales, like a tiny fort, between a bookstore and a shop selling
big wheels of cheese.

'Me?' Scarlett asked, pointing to herself.

'Yes please, Miss. You see, I'm setting out on my own. I've
bought this straw to build a house but I'm not tall enough to
build the roof. Can you help me?' he said, dropping the bale of
hay down and sitting upon it with a sigh. Scarlett was just about
to say that she couldn't, that she was in a rush to get to the
station, but then the pig's bottom lip began to quiver, and his
eyes welled with tears.

'Fine, sure,' she said, walking over to him. 'What do you need?'

'It's just I'm so short,' the pig said. 'I just need a bit of help.
So, if you can find it in your heart, can you build me a small
house? Just a couple of floors. Maybe a basement. And an attic.
Nothing too claustrophobic. I was thinking roomy. Bright.
Spacious. But modern.' The pig smiled up at her hopefully.

'All out of straw?' Scarlett asked, amused.

'Straw is the in thing this year, they say,' he replied confidently.

'I'm sorry, I can't help you do all that. I have to get home. My
dad will be waiting for me. Good luck!' Scarlett said and turned
to head off, just as two other pigs came out of the bookstore and
trotted over to them.

'Who's your new friend?' one of the other pigs called out as
he pulled down his sunglasses to see better. He was wearing pink
tennis shorts with a pink polo top that, like his friend's, didn't
quite meet, leaving a stretch of plump belly between them.

'This is only the finest interior designer in the whole of

Knoware!' the little pig in the sailor suit said, proudly coming up and standing next to her. 'She was just about to build me a cosy – but spacious – modern apartment – all from straw!'

'Straw?' the pig in the tennis outfit asked in surprise. 'That's very last year.'

'Yes,' the third pig said, who was wearing tight jeans, a cowboy hat and a tight red checked shirt – the buttons of which looked as if they might all pop off at any moment. 'Sticks are the new thing according to *What Cottage?* magazine!'

'No, it's bricks that are in!' the pig in the tennis outfit replied.

The pig in the sailor costume changed his expression and looked up at her accusingly. 'Well, that's what I told you, didn't I?'

Just then, the pig in the tennis outfit took off his sunglasses and stared at her feet. She was wearing her red Converse trainers, which looked fine to Scarlett, but the pig was definitely staring at them. Suddenly, he pointed to the ground under her feet with a shaking trotter and squealed as if he had seen a wolf.

What was he looking at? Scarlett immediately looked about her, sure there must be a snake or a giant spider nearby. But there was nothing there. The pig was pointing at the ground beneath her feet and squealing, wide-eyed with terror.

The other two pigs looked confused. Then the pig in the cowboy costume began to squeak too, tugging the pig in the sailor suit's sleeve and pointing to her feet. Scarlett pulled her jeans up and twisted about to look. When she looked back up, all three pigs were now running around each other, squealing and pointing. Then others came up, all sorts of bipedal animals, distracted from their business by all the commotion. At first, they shared confused glances with each other, then there were whispers and gasps and more pointing to the ground.

Again, Scarlett looked down at the path beneath her, but she couldn't see anything – and that suddenly felt wrong, as if she should be noticing something that wasn't there. Then she realised what was missing. She spun around looking for it beneath her feet, but it simply wasn't there. It was impossible, by all the laws of science it was impossible, but her shadow had gone.

Falling to her knees, she held out her arms and moved them about to look for the shadow they must surely cast, but there was nothing there. She looked to the other animals. They all had strong, dark shadows stretching off behind them towards the little pig's bales of hay, but somehow, Scarlett threw no shadow at all.

Panicking, Scarlett scrambled to her feet and ran. At first, she had no direction, no aim, she only wanted to get away from the stares and the pointing. Then, the station. The station. She just had to get back to the station. Once she got on the train and got back to Mournt, where her dad would be waiting for her, she would be back to normal. It was only in this stupid world that she didn't have a shadow. It would surely come back when she got to her world. Without hesitating another second, she hurried straight towards the station, past a duck in a wedding dress, a dog that was selling sausages from a cart and, drinking outside The Three Pigs pub, a giant frog who doffed his cap to her as she hurried by. Undeterred by the polite, but still very strange creatures, Scarlett ran on.

When she turned the final bend of the little lane, the station came into view and there was the train still waiting for her. The station was not at all the same as Mournt's. It did only have one platform like Mournt, but this station's roof rose into a four-sided clock tower. Scarlett could only see two clockfaces, but both were showing different times. She drew in a deep breath and let it go with a relieved smile. Soon she would be back on the train towards Mournt and this whole, horrible nightmare could be forgotten. Running onto the platform, she was shocked at how she could have thought that it was Mournt station that she had woken up in the night before. Somehow the train, with its old, pull-open doors and mahogany-lined interior, didn't look out of place in that strange land. There was no display board on the platform, just a chalk board on the station wall that read: THE TRAIN IS DUE TO LEAVE PRETTY SOON. She didn't care, though. She was going to sit on the train until it pulled out, even if she had to wait all weekend. Scarlett would sleep there if she had to so as not to miss it leaving.

Pulling the handle down and towards her, she opened the train door and she stepped inside. At least, she went to step inside, but it felt as though she didn't fit. Something was pulling her back or blocking her way. She tried going in sideways, then quickly, then by leaning forwards and putting all her weight into it, and then by pushing herself onto the train backwards, but it was no good. It was like that feeling you get when you try to push the same ends of magnets together. The was an invisible force pushing her back.

'Sorry,' a gruff voice said behind her, making her jump. 'You can't board the train without your shadow, Madam. You'll have to find it before boarding.' The voice came from a badger, walking on its hind legs like a human, and dressed in the uniform of an old-fashioned ticket inspector, with a blue cap and blue waistcoat over a white shirt with a smart navy-coloured blazer.

'I don't know where my shadow is. I think I must have left it in my world. If I can just get back, I can find it. I don't belong here. You have to let me on!' Scarlett pleaded.

'You couldn't have got here without your shadow, Madam, could you? Anyway, it's not my decision, is it?' he said, puffing his chest out. 'Those are the rules. You can't just go travelling between worlds without your shadow, can you? Nope. No shadow, no travel.' And with that, the badger strolled off down the platform seeming to forget Scarlett was even there.

'Fine,' Scarlett said, as she stormed off down the track towards a tunnel. If she wasn't going by train, then she'd walk back along the track. She quickly reached the tunnel and set off into the dark towards home. Even though the tunnel was truly black, she wasn't scared, she had just woken up in a room with talking bears, so walking through a dark tunnel was nothing compared to that.

Tapping the rail of the track with her foot so as not to trip over it, and with her left hand on the wall, she was able to walk forwards without falling over. It was a little disconcerting not to be able to see anything ahead, not even a pinprick of light, but she pressed on knowing that to get to the other side would be to put this bad dream behind her. After a while, she stopped to look back and see how far she'd come and was surprised to see that, despite walking for a good while, the entrance to the tunnel was just a few paces behind her. She turned back to face the darkness and walked on, quickening her pace, determined to get as far away from Knoware as possible.

After a careful but brisk pace, Scarlett glanced back. Again, the entrance was still there, just a couple of steps behind her. Not bothering to tap her foot along the rail anymore, she started to run. After a few paces she didn't even bother to put her hand on the wall to orientate herself in the blackness. She was sprinting as fast as she could, the gravel scrunching under her feet in total darkness knowing that she could smack straight into the tunnel wall or trip over the tracks at any moment. She ran and ran until her heart was thumping and her lungs burned. Coming to a stop, she stood, hands on hips, panting and turned back to see if she had made any distance. She let out an agonised groan when the tunnel entrance was still there, just a good jump away.

Her legs gave way and Scarlett, close to tears, dropped onto the floor. She would be trapped there forever.

4

Blondie

'HEY,' A TIMID VOICE ECHOED ALL around her in the tunnel mouth. Looking up, Scarlett saw a girl about her own age standing in the entrance to the tunnel with a deep-red rose clipped into her curly, blonde hair. She was wearing high-waisted jeans, a white t-shirt and a denim jacket with chunky white Reebok trainers on her feet. Scarlett stood up and adjusted her jacket, trying to smarten herself up. The girl glanced up at her every now and then but mostly kept her gaze on her own feet, her jaw working from side to side as she chewed her gum and nervously twisted her golden hair with one hand, careful not to knock the flower above her ear.

'Alright,' the girl said, in little more than a whisper. 'You're not from round here, are you?'

'No,' Scarlett answered, finding her voice and wiping her tears away on the sleeve of her jacket. 'I'm Scarlett. I'm from the real world.'

The other girl flashed a smile before she looked down again, her face impassive. 'I'm Blondie,' the girl said, wincing, as if saying her name was painful. 'Apparently my mum named me after some band in the 80s. I hate it. And, this world's real too, but I know what you mean,' she finished, offering a floppy hand for Scarlett to shake. Scarlett walked forward and shook it. 'I heard all the fuss the pigs were making, and they told me that you'd come this way. It's rare to find a human in Knoware,' Blondie said, taking her hand back.

'I was trying to get back through the tunnel. Is that how you got here?' Scarlett asked, turning and staring into the blackness.

'No. A story for another time, maybe,' Blondie said, putting both hands in her pockets. 'It's really not that interesting, actually,' she finished, tailing off and staring at the ground.

'How long have you been here then?' Scarlett asked, just excited to see another human being.

'I don't know,' Blondie said, shrugging. 'Time works differently here, I reckon. Sometimes it feels like I've only been here a few days. Other times, it feels like I've been here forever. It's hard to tell. Every day is the same. Always summer. I've never had a haircut and my hair's never got any longer. My shoes still fit, and I've still got the same piece of gum in my mouth. But I might have been here years.'

'But don't you want to get back? Won't anyone be missing you?'

'Not really. I think I remember being pleased when I found this place.'

'Blondie, what year was it when you came here?' Scarlett asked, a suspicion forming in her mind.

'Nineteen-ninety-two. Why? What year is it now?' Blondie asked.

'It's two thousand-and-twenty! You've been here ... ' Scarlett did some quick, mental calculations.

'Wow,' Blondie said, 'I've been here forty years!'

'No, that's twenty-eight years!'

'Oh, okay. Well, I still don't feel that old.'

'You're not. You look twelve', and Scarlett looked about her at the trees in the distance and the wildflowers all around the tunnel entrance, bright red poppies and mauve foxgloves, all of them perfect and unblemished. Not a single withered leaf or petal could be seen. 'Maybe nothing gets older in Knoware? Can you help me get back? My dad will be going mad if I'm not at the station soon and then mum will find out and then things will really kick off.'

'You're not going anywhere without your shadow, are you?' Blondie said, pointing to the ground. 'I would give you mine, but she took my shadow too,' she said and pointed to the shadowless ground around her. 'Not that I need mine. I don't want to go back, do I?'

'What do you mean?' Scarlett asked.

'The old lady. She took yours too, right?'

And in a split second Scarlett realised what had happened on the bridge and she felt as though she might be sick. Her legs wobbled and she found herself sitting on the ground. 'The old lady! She cut off my shadow.'

Blondie nodded. 'Yep. That would be Crimsin.'

'Who's Crimson?' Scarlett asked, numb with shock.

'Crim-sin,' Blondie corrected. 'Crimsin is about the only thing you have to worry about in this world, well, in this village at least. She's the wicked witch, the evil queen, the foul stepmother. She created or commands everything bad or dangerous in this world. Crimsin made what lives under the bridge and what lurks in the dark of the forest and what waits in a cottage made of marzipan in the middle of the woods. But you don't have to worry about her. Now she's got your shadow, she and her beasts will leave you alone, I reckon. She got what she wanted. Your shadow is the price you pay to live here', and she began to walk off, before pausing and turning back as if remembering something. 'Want to come play bowls with the ducks?' she asked.

'No!' Scarlett said, exasperated.

'I don't blame you. They're terrible losers', and she carried on walking off, hands still dug deep in her pockets, as though that had concluded the conversation.

'But I don't want to live here. This is all a mistake. A misunderstanding. I have to get it back. I need my shadow! She stole it!' Scarlett protested, running after her.

'Listen, you do what you want, but if you go off to find Crimsin, you won't be coming back,' Blondie said, flicking her golden locks behind her ears and adjusting the rose in her hair. 'You'll be fine, eventually, when you start to forget. You must have asked to come here.'

Scarlett stared at the ground, despair threatening to engulf her as she remembered her unsent text, but she squashed it down and ran after Blondie again.

'Can you tell me where I can find her then?' she asked her.

'Who, Crimsin? You're crazy. But you can find her through the forest,' Blondie replied. 'Through the woods and over the lake then through the forest then who knows where.'

Scarlett stopped and looked around at the endless trees that encompassed the fields about them on all sides. 'Which direction?'

'Trust me, you don't want to get any closer to Crimsin than you are right now. Just forget about your shadow and getting back home,' Blondie said, glancing around. 'This place is alright. No one to hassle you, friendly animals. You could do a lot worse.'

'I have to get home,' Scarlett sighed, clenching her fists and stomping after her. 'My dad is waiting for me.'

Blondie shrugged apologetically. 'Don't you think I'd have gone and got my shadow back ages ago if it were that easy.'

Being too despondent to talk any more, Scarlett simply followed her companion in silence across the meadow and through a huge field of golden-brown corn that moved in the wind like a flock of starlings wheeling about the sky. Soon, they were back at the outskirts of Hapglade and the smell of freshly baked bread started Scarlett's tummy rumbling.

As they passed the mill and the blacksmith's, the village became busier and busier until they came to the central open square. 'Where do you live? Do you have a house in the village?' Scarlett asked, finally breaking the silence.

'No, I only come to the village now and then to stock up,' Blondie said. 'Sometimes crash at the Three Bears' place, but the beds are always so hard there. We don't get on so well!' and she walked up to a market stall selling fruits and vegetables where Scarlett joined her.

'Hello, my darling,' said the rosy-cheeked sheep that was tending the stall to her. 'How's your grandmother? Is she any better?'

'Huh?' Scarlett asked, thinking that the sheep must have been speaking to Blondie, but when she looked up when Blondie didn't reply, she realised the sheep was talking to her.

'Your grandmother, who lives in the forest? She wasn't feeling well, was she?'

'Have you two met before?' Blondie asked.

'Oh, right, yeah!' Scarlett said, spotting an opportunity. 'Grandma is really ill. So ill. Really needs fruit, I think.'

'Well, let me put together a little basket for you then,' the sheep said, picking up a wicker basket and filling it with apples, strawberries, blackberries, carrots and a lettuce.

'No, you don't have to do that,' Scarlett protested, although not very strongly, as she took the basket from the sheep. 'Hopefully she will feel better after this.'

The sheep blushed and put a hoof up to her chest, clearly moved by Scarlett's words.

'What was she on about?' Blondie asked as they walked off and turned a corner. 'How is your Grandmother here too?'

'I have no idea,' Scarlett said with a grin. 'She must think I look like some other girl, but I could be onto a winner here. I could come back every day and she looks stupid enough to keep giving me fruit baskets!'

'Hey, that's not cool, Scarlett. These animals don't deserve

that. They're so kind and dopey, it's not fair. Like, you know
how you can pretend to throw a ball for a dog, and it will still
run after it, even if it's the twentieth time in a row you pretend.
That's like these animals. And their memories are awful. Like,
they can't remember what happened last month, and they'll
believe anything, so don't take advantage, please,' Blondie begged.

'I'm sorry!' Scarlett said sarcastically, with more venom than
she felt. She was used to people laughing along with her and
egging her on when she'd steal things.

'Anyway, I thought you were leaving.'

'I am,' Scarlett said, shaking her head clear to focus again.
'Every minute I'm here, though, my life on the other side of the
tunnel seems more like a dream and this seems more and more
real. I really need to get my shadow back, don't I?'

'Well, good luck. Maybe I'll see you around,' Blondie said
without a backwards look as she skulked off between the cake
maker's and a hatter's. Scarlett kicked a stone off down the road.
She'd managed to upset the one human who seemed to live in
this world with her.

What did she do now? Looking around her at the strangeness
of the animals walking about she felt like screaming and running
in any direction, but there was a cool part of her mind that
pulled her back from the cliff edge. Go back to the three bears'
house, she thought. As weird and dangerous as it was, it was the
only thing she knew in this world. She'd go back there and think.

She walked out of the square and after a few minutes of brisk
walking she recognised The Three Pigs pub and found her way
back to the The Bears' Bed & Breakfast.

Shutting the gate behind her, she made her way up the path and sheepishly knocked on the door. Almost immediately the door opened.

'Hello, dear. We didn't expect to see you back. Did you miss your train?' Mummy Bear said, opening the door wider and standing to one side so that she could come in.

'They wouldn't let me on the train. No shadow, see,' Scarlett said, and pointed to the shadowless space beneath her feet.

'Oh, darling,' Mummy Bear said, pulling her into a hug. 'What happened?'

And the emotional flood gates suddenly opened, and Scarlett began to sob. Through gasps and sniffs and unintelligible bouts of gibberish, she told Mummy Bear what had happened. After stroking Scarlett's hair, Mummy Bear guided her into the kitchen and sat her down on a chair that was far too big for her and made her a nice pot of tea, which Mummy Bear assured her would make it all better.

Scarlett explained everything: how she had wished never to see her dad again as she got on the train, waking up in Knoware, meeting the old lady, losing her shadow, upsetting Blondie, although she didn't explain why. Her sobs slowed until she was more in control and only the odd sniff or sharp intake of breath interrupted her story.

'And tomorrow, if I'm allowed to stay here one more night, I'm going to set off to Crimsin and get my shadow back,' Scarlett finished with a nod. Crying it all out had seemed to sharpen things in her mind, as if her task had suddenly come into focus. 'I know if I stay here too long, I'll stay forever. So, can I stay just one more night? I'll leave a great review.'

'Of course you can stay another night, my dear. But getting to Crimsin won't be easy. She lives in a castle way past the forest. We bears don't tend to wander far into that forest anymore and you're a lot shorter and less scary than a bear,' Mummy Bear said.

'I don't see how I have any choice. If I want to get back home, then first I have to face Crimsin and get my shadow back from her!'

'Then we'll do all we can to help. You can stay the night here and be well rested for your adventure.'

And so Mummy Bear began busying herself about the kitchen preparing her a hamper of food to take with her. Meanwhile, Scarlett picked up her backpack and headed upstairs, determined to come up with some kind of plan. It wasn't going to be easy just on her own, with no idea of where she was, or where she was going, or even what she would do if she met Crimsin. After looking through her bags and her pockets to see what she had, she started to grow a little despondent. She wanted a compass and a water flask and a hunting knife, but instead she had three fountain pen cartridges, some spare underwear and a bottle of conditioner. Writing a list always made her feel more confident, but after an hour of thinking, her to-do list consisted of one entry: FIND CRIMSIN. In fact, the more she thought about it, the more hopeless it all seemed to her. By the time Mummy Bear called her down for supper, Scarlett's initial enthusiasm had almost entirely drained away and she almost felt like giving up again.

Head low, she trudged downstairs and sat down, just as Daddy
Bear and Baby Bear came through the door.

'Ah, you're back. Couldn't get enough of the place, right?'

'It sure is the best bed-and-breakfast I've stayed at,' Scarlett
said, trying to sound cheery.

Mummy Bear updated Daddy Bear on everything that had
happened so far as they all sat down to eat. It was soup followed
by a tasty pie, which the bears ate very daintily with silver
cutlery.

'Well,' said Daddy Bear, 'if you're still insistent on going,
then have a look in this box', and so saying, he swept aside the
crockery to one edge of the table and lifted up a huge wooden
chest that he brought down from on top of a cupboard. 'These
are all the things that travellers and adventurers that have stayed
here before have left behind, forgotten, or given in payment and
we no longer want.' Daddy Bear blew the dust off its top,
unclipping the latch and then opening the lid for Scarlett to see.
'You can take whatever you think will be useful.'

Scarlett knelt on her chair and looked inside the wooden box.
There was an assortment of odds and ends. There was a gold
bracelet, which normally she would have pocketed at once, but
now didn't seem so important. There was also a comb, an old
cassette tape that read NOW THAT'S WHAT I CALL MUSIC VOLUME 7
which made her heart sink as it reminded Scarlett of her dad
who had a stack of them in a shoebox under his bed. As silly as it
was, she wanted to take it just to feel closer to him, to give it as
a gift to him when she saw him next, but she didn't. She picked
up a faded blue hand mirror. Holding it up to look at herself,

she gasped. She was beautiful. No puffy eyes, or crazy hair – she looked energised and sparkly and her hair was perfectly cut. Then she realised that her reflection was grinning a perfect smile back at her, even though she wasn't smiling herself.

'You can do this, Scarlett. I just know you can!' her reflection said to her and Scarlett almost dropped the mirror in shock. Fortunately, she caught it in time and saw that the other side had a mirrored surface. Looking into this side, she expected to see the same thing, but it wasn't at all. Her reflection in this side looked awful. Her eyes were bloodshot with dark bands beneath them, her skin was dry and blotchy, and her hair was wild and messy.

'Give up, Scarlett. What are doing? You can't just go wandering off in the forest looking for danger!' Scarlett spun the mirror around to see the healthy, glowing reflection. 'You've got this!' it said to her with a knowing smile.

'What is this?' Scarlett asked, turning the mirror backwards and forwards in her hands.

'It's a looking glass, darling,' Mummy Bear said in the patronising tone she had used before when explaining how trains worked.

'But it shows me in two different ways,' she said, and handed the mirror to Mummy Bear who held out a paw to take it. Mummy Bear turned the mirror over and over, staring into both sides.

'They both look the same to me, but then, you humans are complicated things. You think one thing and yet say another or say one thing and do something else entirely. We bears do and say what we think. Maybe there's not another side of us to show,' Mummy Bear said, handing the mirror back.

'I'll take it!' Scarlett said, not sure how it would be useful yet, but she knew it was magical and that must count for something. She put it into her backpack and looked at what else was in the chest. There was some string, a towel and a few other odds and ends, but, apart from a crude, hand-drawn map of Knoware that she took, nothing else looked very useful.

'Thank you for everything you've done. I just wish there was something I could do in return,' Scarlett said, putting the map and mirror into her backpack.

Baby Bear eyed her fingers and licked his lips.

5

The Journey out of Hapglade

AS THE FIRST RAYS OF SUNSHINE spilt through her gingham curtains, Scarlett leapt out of bed and got dressed as the sweet smell of porridge rose up from downstairs. By the time Scarlett had pulled on her red jacket, new smells of freshly cooked toast floated from the kitchen below. Cutlery was being clattered against crockery and the old grandfather clock downstairs struck seven. Pulling the curtains apart, she opened the window and leant on the sill. The pig she had seen the day before was in the same spot, resting against the wall, dressed in his golf clothes. He was smoking his pipe, which he kept rested in his mouth, as he struggled with a newspaper. On seeing her, though, he folded the paper under his arm and doffed his cap in greeting before making his way down the street, whistling a tune to himself.

Scarlett found herself taking up the pig's tune as she closed the window and made her way downstairs, whistling as she went. The three bears were already sitting down with crumb covered plates and used bowls strewn about the table. A chair had been left for her and she pulled it out and sat down between Mummy Bear and Baby Bear. Daddy Bear was buttering toast with a butter knife which he held clumsily in his giant fist whilst Mummy Bear poured fresh tea for everyone.

'Good morning, petal. How are you feeling?' Mummy Bear asked as she dabbed at her jaws with a napkin.

'Fresh as a daisy,' Scarlett said, taking some toast.

Conversation was light and she made sure to compliment the room and the bed as often as she could. She ate quickly, trying to keep her fingers away from Baby Bear, and thanked them all again for everything they had done for her. Then she got up to leave.

Mummy Bear insisted on giving her a bear hug before she left and then all the three bears came to the door with her to wave her off and give her a basketful of provisions – fruits, a roll and slab of cheese wrapped in wax paper, for which Scarlett thanked them again and again. Swinging open the front door, she was greeted by a warm breeze, heavy with the scent of roses and honeysuckle, and also by someone waiting for her at the end of the garden path. Leaning against a tree on the other side of the white picket fence, a rose in her golden hair and her hands in her pockets, was Blondie.

'Hey,' Blondie said, giving a small, almost imperceptible, upwards movement of her head in way of greeting.

'Hey. What are you doing here?' Scarlett asked, as she sauntered over.

'Oh! You! Don't I know you!' Daddy Bear shouted from the doorway.

'Quick, walk faster,' Blondie said, taking her by the arm and hurrying away, pretending she hadn't heard. 'Normally these animals forget everything after a month or so, but he still hasn't forgiven me for running out that first time.'

Scarlett smiled. 'I thought I was going to get eaten a few times. I nearly ran for it too.'

'You still want to find Crimsin?' Blondie asked as they headed through the central square, then down a small cobbled lane with stone cottages on either side.

'Yes!' Scarlett said, smiling wider.

'You going to start being nicer to the animals?'

'Yeah, listen. You've got me all wrong. That wasn't me yesterday. Well, not the real me. I'll show you,' Scarlett said excitedly.

Blondie shrugged. 'Okay. We'll see, I guess. Finding Crimsin won't be easy though! They say there are things in the forest that shouldn't be disturbed.'

'I have to try,' Scarlett said, and then remembered the mirror in her backpack. 'Hey, you want to see something really cool?' and, swinging her backpack off her shoulder as she walked, she took out the looking glass. First, Scarlett looked at the cracked side. 'Watch.'

'Scarlett, how do you know we can trust this stranger? You're better off on your own! Don't be so needy!' Scarlett's pained and tired reflection said from the cracked side of the mirror.

'Sorry! I don't think that,' Scarlett apologised, quickly putting the mirror down to her side before her reflection could say anything else.

'Yes, you do, Scarlett. Mirrors don't lie,' Blondie said. 'Even magic ones! If you want to go on your own, be my guest!'

'Wait, there's another side,' Scarlett called out as Blondie began to walk off.

'Wow! What an amazing friend you've found. She came back for you when no one else was there. She's giving you another chance. Hang on to this one!' her glowing reflection said from the other side of the mirror.

'See, that's what I really think!' Scarlett shouted. Blondie slowed down and sheepishly looked up.

'You really think that?' Blondie asked.

'I do. I really do. You didn't have to come back, and I know I annoyed you, but you're the only other human around here. You're as close as home as I can get for the moment,' Scarlett said, shifting around uncomfortably.

'Can I look in the mirror?' Blondie asked. 'I've seen magic mirrors before, but not two-faced ones.'

'Sure,' Scarlett said, handing it over and stepping behind Blondie to see what she saw.

Blondie's face appeared in the image, rosy-cheeked and perfect. 'What a good friend you are, looking out for someone else. I think you two are going to be best friends,' Blondie's perfect reflection said. Blondie turned the mirror around.

'Typical you. You're too scared to face what a disaster your life is, so now you're going to latch on to the one person in this world whose life might actually be more messed up than yours,' Blondie's drawn and tired reflection said with a look of real disappointment and disgust.

'Wow, that really sounded like my inner monologue,' Blondie said, handing the mirror back with the raise of one eyebrow. 'You think that mirror is going to help?'

'Not a clue. Seemed fun though,' Scarlett said with a shrug and slid the mirror in her backpack.

By this time the two girls were nearing the edge of Hapglade and Scarlett was feeling positive. She found herself whistling the theme tune to *The Smurfs* and wondered why that song should pop into her head, when suddenly there was a commotion from a few streets away. Raised voices could be heard and the girls, in silent agreement, went to see what the fuss was all about.

As they turned the corner, they came up behind a dog who was talking to someone in front of it. The dog was dressed as a policeman and was at least six-foot-tall wearing its old English policeman's helmet and walking around quite naturally on two legs. The person he was telling off, though, was completely hidden from view.

'You're not welcome here, you know that. Not after the mess you made,' said the policeman, chastising the unknown person in front of him in a nasally, measured pace.

'The mess wasn't as bad as people made out. Not once it had all been scraped up and everything had been given a good wash,' the hidden figure in front of the police dog said in a gruff, female voice that was trying to sound light and cheery.

'The smell of that incident still lingers in my police kennel! Now, be off with you!' And with that, the police dog turned and walked away through the crowd of other animals. He was a Bassett Hound with long, brown ears and droopy eyelids, and he picked his way through the crowd leaving the figure of a small woman walking slowly away from town down a tree-lined track.

As the woman was going the same way as they were, they soon caught up with her. After seeing her face, though, Scarlett was reminded of someone and it took her a few seconds to work out who it was. This tiny woman reminded her of Heather, the lady who ran the chip shop around the corner from her mum's house. Heather was a stern looking woman and she and Scarlett had been involved in many run-ins. In their last encounter, Heather had chased her, showing remarkable stamina for a woman her size and age, for almost a mile. The whole incident had been blown out of proportion, of course. She recollected it had something to do with a can of Fanta that disappeared up Scarlett's sleeve on the unspoken understanding that she would pay for it on some future occasion when she had some money. Then horrible names were exchanged and chips, Scarlett blushed to remember, may have been thrown, and the chase began. Although the finer details of the incident eluded her, she never forgot Heather's sweaty face as she chased her around the estate.

'What you staring at? Come to gawp, have you?' the little woman asked, her chubby face blotchy, and her brown eyes ringed with red where she was crying.

'No, sorry,' Scarlett mumbled and looked forward. 'You just reminded me of – an old friend.'

'Oh,' she said, rolling up the sleeves of her white top that had the slogan WHERE'S NEIL WHEN YOU NEED HIM? emblazoned across

the front. Scarlett couldn't help but feel that a top with writing
on looked out of place in Knoware, yet this woman didn't strike
her as being quite human either. Sure, at first, she had looked
just like Heather from the chip shop who was, as far as Scarlett
knew, human. But the longer you looked at her, the less human
she looked. For instance, her ears seemed to wiggle and move a
lot when she spoke. Her chubby face seemed too expressive,
almost cartoon-like at times.

'What was all that about back there?' Scarlett asked, conscious
that she was staring.

'I'm being kicked out because people are scared of my magical
powers, aren't I!' the woman replied.

'No, you're not. They're kicking you out because your
"potion"', and here Blondie added air quotes around the word
potion, 'made everyone ill.'

'They were all complaining of earache. No one complained
of an earache after they took my potion, did they?' the little
woman said with a satisfied nod, taking a red and white spotted
handkerchief out of the pocket of her shorts and dabbing at her
forehead.

'No, because they were all moaning about the diarrhoea you'd
given them instead!' Blondie said, accusingly.

'Still worked. Magic is never straightforward. Never what you
expect,' the gruff woman said, putting her hanky away and waving
her fingers in the air as if trying to create an air of mystique.

Blondie rolled her eyes and she and Scarlett picked up the
pace to push ahead. The cottages of Hapglade were far behind
them and only golden fields of corn with a few farmhouses

scattered about stood between them and the woods on the horizon. There were trees either side of the road, and although the ripe corn told Scarlett it was late summer, all the trees were in blossom, reds and pinks and whites like a park in Japan in the springtime. The only problem was that the little woman was storming off too and now all three of them were power walking faster and faster to move ahead, but all only succeeded in keeping pace with each other. When they realised what was happening, they all slowed down together too, and it made for a most awkward few moments.

'Where are you going? Hopefully we won't have to share a path for long,' Scarlett said, feeling that her grand undertaking had got off to a very strange and strained start.

'None of your business where I'm going,' the lady said, and crossed her arms as she marched along. 'Where are you going?'

'We're going to find Crimsin,' Blondie said, getting in first before Scarlett could reply that it was none of the woman's business either.

'Why do you want to go there? Want to get turned into something nasty?' the woman asked.

'I'm going to get my shadow back,' Scarlett said, pointing to her feet.

'Oh. Oh dear. She didn't happen to cut your shadow away with a pair of fine-looking silver scissors, did she?' the woman asked cautiously.

Scarlett nodded. 'She did. I assume that wasn't just a lucky guess?'

'Oh dear, oh dear. This is all my fault!' the little woman stammered and then, quite suddenly and violently, stopped walking and began to cry.

At first, all that Scarlett could do was stop too and stare in shock as the woman wailed that it was all her fault over and over again.

Putting an arm around her, Scarlett made appropriate shushing noises and looked to Blondie for help who just shrugged back. 'Why is this all your fault?' she asked.

It took a long time for the woman to calm down enough to talk. 'They were my Lady's scissors, passed down to her from her grandmother and her grandmother before her, right down from the first fairy queen of Knoware', and here she burst into violent sobbing again. 'They had been in the royal family's possession for two hundred thousand years and I was left to look after them for five minutes and Crimsin stole them from me!' She paused a number of times during this speech to blow her nose on her spotted hanky before dabbing at her forehead again. 'They kicked me out – banished me from the Fay-Lands.'

Scarlett patted the woman's shoulders. 'If they were that important, why did you have them?'

'It was my duty that day to take the scissors from the royal treasury to the castle. My order are the only ones trusted with such a job. I was so proud, I was. I thought that maybe I could go and show my friends so they could see I wasn't a total failure. They'd never believe me unless they saw me with them, I thought. Only, I got a little bit distracted on my way to see them and bought a pie and then got a bit tired and then maybe had a nap and then ... ' but she burst out crying again before she could finish.

Scarlett looked thoughtful for a moment, 'Do you think they would let you back in if you got the scissors back?'

'Maybe,' the woman said with a sniff. 'But it's not like Crimsin is just going to hand them over, is she?'

'No, but if I'm going to get our shadows back, then we may as well get your scissors back too!' Scarlett said with a defiant nod.

The little woman looked up at her though her tears. 'And you're really going to get them back?'

'Well, I'm going to try,' Scarlett said.

'Really?' the little woman asked in disbelief.

'Yes. I'm going to find her and get my shadow back, and Blondie's too, if she wants it. And your scissors as well.'

'Then we'll go together. I will lend my services to you on our quest,' the woman said, straightening herself up and wiping her tears away.

'And what services are those?' Scarlett asked.

'Well, all the powers a fairy of the high order possesses, of course,' she said, standing up straight and proud, almost to Scarlett's shoulder.

Scarlett blinked and shook her head at this as if she hadn't heard correctly. 'You're a fairy?'

'Yes,' the woman said proudly.

'Sorry. Just to clarify. A fairy?' Scarlett asked again, sure she had misheard.

'Yes!' the woman repeated, looking less than impressed now.

'Why is that so hard to believe?'

Scarelett looked her up and down. The large, socked feet in the opened-toed sandals, the short, hiker's legs and tight shorts, sweaty red face and hair scraped back into a ponytail. 'Well,' Scarlett started, not quite sure what to say. 'You're certainly taller than I imagined. I thought fairies were supposed to be ... '

'What?' the little woman asked.

'Smaller', and Scarlett indicated with her hands about how small she thought a fairy might be. 'With wings and stuff. And they could fly.'

'Fly! A flying fairy!' the woman exclaimed and burst into raucous laughter for far longer than was comfortable. Her cheeks turned red and she doubled over until even standing was too much for her and she fell to a heap on the floor.

After waiting a polite amount of time, Scarlett and Blondie walked on, leaving the fairy laughing away. She soon noticed they had moved on and, with some effort, she got back to her feet and began to waddle after them.

Scarlett and Blondie stopped and waited for her to catch up whilst Scarlett took the map from her bag and studied it. Chewing her lip, she looked around for landmarks to find her position on the map.

'What's your name?' Scarlett asked absentmindedly as she continued to study the map.

The fairy had to take two deep breaths and wipe the tears from her eyes before she could answer. 'The other fairies call me Inutilia Mediocris, which means Great Powerful One, but you can call me Tilia for short.'

'Right. Tilia, welcome to our group,' Scarlett said and shook her plump little hand. 'We're just planning our route.'

'We're here,' Blondie said, leaning over and confidently pointing to a spot on the map. 'If we want to get to Crimsin's castle, which is way up here, we need to go north. If we can carry straight on for a day or so we can try to cross Tears Lake. If we can't cross the lake, we're looking at a journey downstream to cross the river at this bridge and then a two-day journey across the Needle Mountains, so we need to get across that lake somehow. Then we go through Darkthorn Woods, across the Luz Mala Marshes, then just to the north of here, past the town of Bitterfall, is Crimsin's castle.'

Impressed, Scarlett nodded and looked to Tilia for confirmation but, with tears of restrained laughter streaming down her face and mouthing the words 'flying fairy', Tilia offered no such confirmation.

Ignoring her and walking on, Blondie led the way with the map in front of her, Scarlett in the middle and Tilia holding her sides and waddling behind them.

'I get it – fairies don't fly,' Scarlett said sharply.

'No, of course we don't. We're not even very good at walking. We're terrific sitters though. And masterful at laying down.'

'Lying down,' Scarlett said instinctively, correcting her.

Patches of mauve harebell and bright yellow kingcup grew underneath the blossom sprinkled trees next to the path they followed through the golden fields of wheat towards the treeline that grew before them. The three of them paused as they came to the edge of the fields and the start of the forest – a giant wall of trees from horizon to horizon. Chestnut, oak and ash trees grew so close together they created a thick canopy of dark green that meant barely a ray of sunshine hit the forest floor.

'Well, I guess we're going in,' Scarlett said, not at all wanting to go any further. 'Maybe I should consult the mirror though,' she said, knowing already what it would probably say, but somehow wanting to hear it out loud. She took the two-sided looking glass out of the bag and stared into the cracked side first where her haggard reflection stared back.

'It wasn't enough for you to be travelling with that girl, now you've teamed up with a giant fairy! What a band of useless misfits!'

Scarlett turned the mirror around where her reflection smiled back at herself with perfect teeth and skin that looked fresh and radiant.

'You're not alone anymore. You have two wonderful companions to travel with. Safety in numbers. You can lead them to glory, Scarlett!'

She nodded and put the mirror back in her bag. 'Ok, let's go!' and the three of them set off into the shadow of the trees.

6

The Wolf

IT WAS IMMEDIATELY COOLER INSIDE THE canopy of trees where dappled pea-green light filtered through the dusty haze. They were walking at a good pace, and carried on going, much to Tilia's grumbling, through lunchtime until evening, following the well-worn dirt path.

'So, obviously you don't fly. But, and don't start laughing again, can you do magic?' Scarlett asked.

'Of course,' Tilia said,

'What magic can you do?' Scarlett asked.

Tilia scratched her head and looked about her. 'Thousands of spells. Between me and my sister, there wasn't a spell we didn't know.'

'Can you make me a magic sword? Something to fight Crimsin with when we find her?'

'My sister knew that spell.'

Scarlett sighed. 'Fine, what about a magic item then, one that can help guide us there?'

'No, no, no. The Fairy Code is very strict on this point. It prevents me from making magical items of any kind unless, as it states, page eighteen, paragraph eight, it is *gravely* needed,' Tilia said, wagging her finger to no one in particular.

'What about the magic potion you made for the village? That wasn't life or death,' Blondie asked.

'Ah, now that wasn't really magic. That was more like experimental cooking.'

'Right. What about a spell to speed us up?' Scarlett asked.

'My sister knew that one too,' Tilia said with an apologetic shrug.

'Tilia, is there any situation at all, any, in which you can perform any type of magic, ever?' Scarlett asked.

'Yes, but honestly, it's a legal minefield. Sometimes it's just safer not to try,' Tilia shrugged.

'So, you're a fairy that doesn't fly or do any kind of magic?'

'Oh look! A clearing!' Tilia said, conveniently avoiding the question.

Continuing towards the light, they came out of the forest at the edge of a huge lake. On their left, towards the west, the lake stretched on beyond view into steep cliffs that quickly grew into snow-capped mountains which were reflected in the stillness of the lake below.

'We're not getting around Tears Lake that way,' Tilia said, looking at the mountains. 'I doubt we could even climb those rock faces, and I've heard talk of mountain giants in those parts.'

Opposite them they could make out the other side where they needed to get to, but it would have been a long, tough swim. To their right, Tears Lake continued for a long way before it started to thin out into a broad river. According to the map, if they couldn't find a way across, that was the long route they would have to take.

'Can we swim it?' Scarlett asked hopefully.

'Can't swim,' Blondie said. 'Never learnt.'

'Let me see what the mirror says,' Scarlett said, getting the looking glass out from her backpack.

'You can swim across, Scarlett; you can do it with Blondie holding onto you. You did get your fifty-metre swimming badge, didn't you?' her healthy, grinning self said with a reassuring wink from the mirror.

'I'm not sure I could,' Scarlett said, looking up at the lake. It had to be at least a mile across still. She spun the looking glass around.

'Of course, you can't swim across it, Scarlett,' her sunken-eyed-self said. 'Are you stupid? You wouldn't last a minute on that choppy surface. And what's swimming around in there? More than fish I'd guess.'

'I'm afraid I have to agree with negative me,' Scarlett said to the others. 'We better find another way around.'

'Look!' Blondie said, pointing to the lake shore. Fifty or so yards in front of them was a jetty next to a small thatched cottage. A rowing boat was tied up to a short wooden pole at the end of the wooden pier. The little boat sat quite peacefully in the water, being lapped by gentle waves.

'This is perfect!' Scarlett said. 'Cutting straight across the lake will save us two or three days of walking.'

'Looks too perfect to me,' Blondie said as they all took a step towards the boat. Suddenly, the boat shook and began to jolt and rock. They quickly sprang back into the shadows of the trees to watch. A wolf sat up inside the rowing boat and yawned, giving them a great view of what an enormous mouth it had – big enough to swallow any of them whole. Scarlett felt a tightening in her tummy. The wolf looked like the other animals from the village – it had hands and feet and a black waistcoat and top hat, but something about it made her start to shake. A single child's shoe lay discarded next to the boat on the jetty making Scarlett's heart start to race. The wolf sniffed the air and snapped his head around to face the patch of trees where they hid, his eyes twinkling.

'Hello there,' he called out jovially from the boat, sniffing the air again. 'Don't be scared. Come and join me for a row about the lake. Or pop into my little cottage with me. I could put something nice on for tea.'

There was no temptation to go. He sounded sincere but his eyes flashed malice.

The three of them all stayed silent, trying to breathe as quietly as possible. None of them moved to run or even to take their eyes from the wolf.

'I don't suppose there's any way we can get him away from the boat?' Scarlett whispered.

'Maybe if he's eating one of us then the other two can get on the boat?' Tilia whispered.

'Are you volunteering?' Scarlett asked. Tilia didn't reply. 'I didn't think so. Then we should get out of here', and Scarlett stepped backwards in time with the other two, slowly retreating back into the forest.

'Don't go!' the wolf called, stepping out of the boat, hesitant to attack what he couldn't see.

They stepped slowly backwards for a few more paces then Tilia turned and began to sprint away. Scarlett and Blondie followed, running as fast as they could, soon overtaking the stumpy fairy. Between trees, through bushes, over ditches, never slowing down, they ran on. Every so often Scarlett would steal a glance behind her, convinced she could hear the wolf breathing down her neck. Tilia, with surprising speed, was keeping up but tripped over Blondie who had fallen hard onto her front. Scarlett skidded to a stop and ran back to pick them up, heart racing and her breath coming in quick pants.

'I think it's broken,' Blondie said, rolling over and holding her leg.

'It's not broken. You've just bruised it,' Scarlett said, after inspecting it and then helping her and Tilia up.

'Come on!' Tilia said, calling back from up ahead.

'I think we're all right. I don't think he's following us,' Scarlett said between pants, bent over with her hands resting on her knees. 'That's a real pain. Getting across the lake in that boat would have really saved us some time.'

After taking a few seconds to get her breath back, Scarlett looked around in all directions, trying to work out which way was south or north, but it was hopeless.

'This forest is enormous!' Scarlett said, overwhelmed at the sight of trees in every direction as far as the eye could see.

'You have to think differently,' Tilia said, leaning against a big oak, her cheeks flushed red. 'You're from a place of towns and roads and cities and concrete and there are little patches of trees. But here, it's like your world used to be. The whole world is forest and jungle apart from tiny specks of towns here and there.'

'You seem to know a lot about our world,' Scarlett said.

'We fairies have to serve time in all worlds. I lived in your world for about ten years.'

'Wait, there are other worlds?' Scarlett asked.

'There are hundreds of worlds. Each one a slightly distorted reflection of the others.'

Scarlett didn't know quite how much to believe, but there must be at least two worlds. Was it any harder to believe there were hundreds of others?

'And where did you live? What did you do in my world? Didn't you stand out?'

'I managed to fit in in your world without being noticed just fine, thank you, if that's what you're asking. I worked as a librarian in the day and did amateur dramatics in the evenings.'

'Ahh, I see,' said Scarlett, nodding. 'That makes sense. But none of this helps us now, does it? We're still lost, aren't we?'

'No, look. Moss,' Blondie said, rubbing the moss on an oak tree. 'Moss only grows on the north side of the trees. Plus, the sky's lighter over there between the trees, and it's around dinner time, so that's west.'

'How do you know all this?' Scarlett asked.

'I was in the Girl Guides,' Blondie replied. 'You know, until the girls there got nasty and it stopped being an escape.'

'I'm sorry,' Scarlett said, putting an arm around her shoulder. It was true she didn't really know Blondie, but it's what she would have done with Daisy or Lily and it felt natural. Blondie didn't shrug her off.

'It's fine. We're heading this way', and Blondie led them off again through the trees. The sun was beginning to fade to a soft orange and Scarlett felt a chill in the air. It wasn't long before they came to a river that must have been somewhere west of the lake they had been at earlier. It was deep and fast and wide.

They walked west along its bank for a while until they spied a bridge some way off through the trees. It was a long bridge, maybe forty or so yards, that arched over the foaming river. They hung back a while behind a thicket and waited to see if there was any danger. On top of the posts at the start of the bridge sat two crows carved in wood. Since her meeting with Crimsin on the bridge, Scarlett had a newfound suspicion of bridges and Blondie and Tilia seemed to share it. They silently agreed to remain there where they watched and listened to every rustle of the leaves and splosh of water.

'I'm going to go first,' Tilia said, and stood up straight, level with Scarlett's armpit, and strode off towards the bridge with a swagger.

'She's got confidence,' Scarlett said, with a little nod of appreciation, as she lowered her position to watch. Tilia got halfway across the bridge when she stopped and leaned on the railing, looking down beneath it.

'Why is she waiting?' Blondie asked as they both strained to see what she was looking at. It was hard to see from that distance, what with the leaves in the way too, but it looked as though she was talking to someone. After a second or two, though, she walked across to the other side and waved for them to follow.

'Something's not right,' Blondie said. 'Wait here.' Then she stood up and walked over to the bridge leaving Scarlett on her own behind the bushes. Scarlett watched as Blondie walked across to the middle of the bridge and leaned over the edge, talking to someone beneath her. It was impossible to catch the words over the sound of the rushing of the river and the rustling of leaves, but Blondie finished her conversation and crossed the bridge to the other side, waving Scarlett to follow.

Brushing the leaves from her hoodie, she stood up and made her way around the thicket towards the bridge. Standing some way back from the river on the other side the two others watched her. The river had been strong further back the way they had come, but here the riverbed spread out a lot wider and the water lost much of its force, splashing over rocks and bubbling into the blackness beneath the bridge. Steeling herself, she began to march across the wooden bridge.

'Who's that coming across my bridge?' a deep, gurgling voice asked from under her. Scarlett ran to the edge and, leaning on the rail, peered over and saw the top of a bald, scaly head emerging from the shadows beneath the bridge. Two green eyes peered up at her.

Scarlett gulped, and for a moment, words wouldn't come.

'I'm Scarlett,' she said squeakily. 'I'm just crossing to the other side.'

'Your youngest sister told me to wait for your middle sister, as she was much juicer. And your middle sister told me to wait for you because you were the juiciest. So now I've been thinking about food for a good long while and I've got myself mighty hungry.' More of its head emerged from the darkness. It wasn't a crocodile, because it didn't have a long snout and it wasn't human because it didn't have a nose or ears and it wasn't a boulder because it was talking, yet it reminded Scarlett of all three of these things, and it was coming out from under the bridge to eat her. For what looked like a mass of heavy, gnarled muscle it moved quickly and, in a flash, it had swung itself up onto the bridge to face her, the whole construction shaking under Scarlett as it landed.

The troll, because the word fitted the creature best in her mind, stood eight feet tall. He was the shape of a man, but like a man crudely made by a five-year-old out of clay. Lumps and bumps and ridges covered his green-grey flesh. His hands and feet didn't look finished, with three distinct toes on one foot and none on the other.

With trembling hands, Scarlett reached out and grabbed the other side of the bridge to stop herself falling. A part of her felt like a small child and she was reminded of the time her dad scooped her up as she burst into tears at the zoo, a tiger, seeming like the largest animal alive, rising up against the glass onto its hind legs and roaring. But there was no dad and no glass this time.

She didn't even have a weapon, not that Scarlett thought a weapon would do much good. The troll looked as though he could have been hit by an express train and not taken much damage. Running didn't seem like an option either judging by the effortless speed with which he had leapt onto the bridge and, besides, her legs felt like all the bones had been removed and Scarlett thought she would probably just fall to the ground if she tried to run.

'You can't eat me,' Scarlett said, not sure what her plan was, but knew she'd better start talking.

'Oh, and why's that?' the troll said, taking a rusty spoon out from under his armpit. This threw Scarlett for a moment, but she quickly started talking again.

'Because … because, I'm already someone else's lunch!'

'What? Who?' the troll asked, and Scarlett suspected he would have furrowed his eyebrows in confusion if he had had any eyebrows, but he didn't.

'It's not worth getting upset over it. He told me you'd start crying like a baby,' Scarlett continued, an idea forming.

The troll roared in rage. 'Who dares call me a baby and steal my lunch?'

'The wolf. He's waiting for us back at the lake,' Scarlett continued. The troll puzzled on this for a moment.

'So, why are you coming this way?' the troll asked suspiciously. 'The lake is back that way', and he pointed the way they had come with a massive, knobbly finger as big as Scarlett's forearm.

'He. He, erm, said that he was still pretty full from his breakfast, and that we should go for a walk until he was ready for lunch. But that if we were to see a tiny troll on our way, we were to tell it to not eat us as we were promised to the wolf.'

'Tiny troll?' the troll growled. 'Right, we'll see about that!' and with that, he pushed Scarlett out of the way sending her flying off the bridge and into a bush on the other side, as he stormed off the way they had just come.

'Come on, we have to follow him,' Scarlett said, running after the troll.

'After him?' Blondie asked, mouth dropping.

'Yes, trust me!' Scarlett shouted back, following the troll.

Keeping up with an angry troll was not an easy task Scarlett discovered as she and her companions followed the trail of destruction. When they had to stop to rest, though, the troll kept going, shouting and roaring to himself, ripping trees out of his way and kicking boulders as if they were footballs. When they did eventually catch up with him, the troll had just reached the lake's edge. The wolf was staring at the troll as he ran towards him, a look of total confusion on his face.

'You call me tiny? You call me baby? You eat my lunch?' the troll shouted as he threw a large rock at the wolf who ducked inside the boat as it flew just over his head. Not waiting to ask questions, the wolf leapt out of the boat stuttering and stammering. He skidded about on the stones, faster than the troll but nowhere near as strong.

The boat now lay unoccupied exactly where it had been before. Scarlett was the first to run over and duck behind it, hidden from the duelling creatures' view. Blondie and Tilia came running over too, keeping their bodies ducked low.

'Right, are we doing this?' Scarlett asked, not at all sure that they should attempt to steal the boat but not having a better plan.

'Sure,' Blondie said after a pause, and Tilia nodded. They pushed the prow of the boat into the water and Blondie and Tilia jumped in as Scarlett untied the boat from the post it was bound to. The knot was more complicated than it looked, though, and Scarlett had to hook her nails between the folds of rope to loosen it and pull it free. It seemed to take forever and the longer she was left exposed the more frantic she became. As the rope came loose, Scarlett scrambled into the boat, her two companions pulling her in. There were two oars on the bottom of the boat. Blondie picked them up and handed one to Scarlett. She had only ever been canoeing before, though, on the year six school residential trip, so she began to paddle with it not knowing what else to do. Blondie watched her and tried to copy. The solid oak oars were heavy and cumbersome, and after a few seconds of splashing, the girls realised they were doing it wrong. By this time the splashing had caught the attention of the wolf and the troll.

'You idiot!' the wolf cried. 'My lunch is escaping again!'

'My lunch you mean!' the troll bellowed, pushing the wolf out of the way and bounding over towards them.

'Quick, row, row!' Tilia began to scream from the front of the boat.

Between the three of them, they managed to get the oars into their pivots and started pulling at them. Only Scarlett was facing forwards and Blondie was facing backwards, so once they had managed to move off the sand, they just began to slowly turn around in a circle.

'The other way!' Tilia and Blondie bellowed, and Scarlett quickly moved to face the other way, almost losing her oar in the water as she did so. The troll was wading into the water after them. Scarlett and Blondie were frantically pulling at the oars, but hopelessly out of time with each other so that, although they were moving away from land, they did so in jerky, sideways swishes, like a beached fish might wriggle back into the sea.

'Together girls, pull!' Tilia bellowed. 'Pull!'

The girls began to pull in time and move away faster, but the troll was close now – he paused for a second, coiling himself up, and then lunged at the boat.

7

Tears Lake

SCARLETT AND BLONDIE HEAVED WITH ALL their might and the boat just edged out of the troll's reach as he went crashing face first into the lake sending up a huge wave that soaked them all. They didn't care, though. Their hearts were hammering, and their shoulders ached already. Adrenaline kept them going and they only let themselves relax and slacken the pace when they were well out of reach of anything that the troll might choose to throw at them.

'Well done girls!' Tilia said, with a huge sigh, as if she had been pulling the oars herself, rather than just shouting commands. Resting the oars inside the boat for the moment, Scarlett and Blondie took a moment to breathe and inspect the blisters that were already forming on their hands.

'Right. What happened back at the bridge then?' Scarlett asked. 'You two saved your own skins quickly enough!'

'I'm sorry, Scarlett. I panicked. I knew you'd think of something,' Blondie said, not being able to look Scarlett in the eye. There was a pause and then she did make eye-contact. 'I am sorry.'

'That's not cool,' Scarlett said. 'Not cool!'

'I know, I know. I'm just not used to having friends to stick up for. I'll try to be braver.'

'Hey, it's fine. I don't blame you really. Just don't let it happen again. What about you, Tilia?' Scarlett said, turning to the fairy.

'I was actually preparing a very powerful spell,' Tilia said with a serious look.

Scarlett rolled her eyes. 'Sure you were.' She leant back in the boat with her arms behind her head. 'Anyway, Blondie, I got here on a train. How did you end up in Knoware? We may as well hear the story now,' Scarlett asked.

For a second it looked as if Blondie wouldn't answer, then she sighed, shrugged her shoulders and began. 'I can't remember much. Just bits now. Like, I can't remember my parents, I just remember them fighting all the time and not really being there when they weren't fighting. But I remember how I got here clearly still. I'd bunked off school. Some other kids were winding me up again, so I headed to this house that's all abandoned on the corner of our street, number twenty-seven. It was a good place to go if you didn't want to be found. The doors were locked, but one of the windows round the back had the boards pulled away and you could climb inside if you were careful of the broken glass. I thought only I knew about it at first, but after a while, I'd find bottles and other stuff lying around, so I knew other people used it too.

'Anyway, I went upstairs where it was lighter because they hadn't bothered to board those windows up and stayed there until it was starting to get dark. I wasn't going to stay late, but I wanted to scare my parents – not that they even noticed probably. But then I hear voices downstairs. I look over the banister and see a group of really dodgy looking people and they're all smoking and laughing, and I look around and suddenly realise I'm trapped upstairs. I remember wishing I had somewhere where I could go to hide and disappear. Some place that was safe that no one else could find me. So, I go into the next room, which is empty, with all the wallpaper missing and no carpet, but then I see a hole in the brick wall to another room beyond. I thought, maybe I can hide in the next room until morning, so I crawled through into this smaller room. Just another dark, bare room but there's a gap in the wall on the far side of this room too. So, I go through that hole into another room and another and another, feeling safer and safer with every new room I find until I'm crawling through the brickwork and it seems to go on forever and then I'm out through the wall. Only, it's not into a new room this time, or even the outside of the abandoned house on the corner of my street. I've just crawled out of some small fireplace in a cottage. I wander around but there's no one home. I head outside and I don't get too far when I bump into this old lady.'

'Crimsin!' Scarlett said.

'Exactly. I didn't know that then, of course. Just thought she was some old biddy. Still, she said I had wished for this place and here I was and that I had to pay the toll for crossing over. I had to give her my shadow. I said no, of course. Tried to run, but she took it anyway.'

'And now you're going to get your shadow back!' Scarlett said with a determined grin and a nod.

'I guess. Like I said, what have I got to go back to? This is my home now.'

'I know,' Scarlett said, 'But you should still have your shadow. She had no right to take it so we're getting yours back too!'

Scarlett sat up, feeling the strength returning to her arms. The sun had set and the purple of twilight was fading too. A bright half moon illuminated the lake which they had drifted to the centre of.

'I'm too tired to row much more today. Besides, I want to see where we're landing when it's light,' Scarlett said.

'Ok. I'm happy to sleep in the boat. It feels safer than the woods,' Blondie agreed.

Tilia sat up straight and rubbed her face. 'No worries. I'll stay awake for the first shift and we'll swap over in the night. That way we won't drift back to the wolf.'

'Are you sure you can stay awake?' Scarlett asked.

'Of course. I'm going to cast a spell that will refresh me as if I had slept all night,' Tilia yawned.

'Whatever you say. Just wake me up if you start to drift off,' Scarlett said, lying down between the seats with her jacket zipped to the top and her hood up. Blondie squeezed in next to her and it wasn't long before Scarlett was asleep.

Loud snoring eventually woke Scarlett up. Blearily, she opened her eyes and saw Tilia sprawled out across the seat snoring away, drool hanging from her mouth.

'Hey, wake up!' she said, and gave Tilia a nudge.

Tilia started and jumped up. 'I wasn't asleep. I was just resting my eyes!'

'Sure,' Scarlett said, and began to gently shake Blondie. 'Hey, time to get up. It's morning already', and it was then that Scarlett looked about the boat in amazement. They were still on the lake, but the shore had totally vanished. All sight of land had gone in every direction. The opposite side of the lake had been clearly visible the day before, yet now the lake stretched out forever like the surface of a mirror from horizon to horizon. In every direction there was nothing but the perfectly unbroken surface of the lake reflecting the blue, cloudless sky. Not a ripple or even the smallest wave broke the water. Other than the constant blue, the only trace of colour was a flock of white birds that flew in formation way up high, almost out of sight.

'This is super wired,' Scarlett said, picking up her oar and putting it back in the water, creating ripples that spread out from the boat, breaking the perfect surface of the lake. Blondie took up her oar as well and they both began to row.

After a minute or so, Scarlett stopped rowing and tilted her head to one side. Blondie carried on rowing but stopped too when she saw Scarlett listening. Scarlett heard it again. A whimpering sound, like that of a lonely puppy, drifted across the lake, but it was hard to tell from which direction. Putting her oar down, Scarlett turned around to see where the noise was coming from. Climbing over Tilia's seat, she leant against the prow to get a better view. In front of them, breaking up the impossible stillness of the water, a dark shape rose out of the lake, the only blemish on the horizon.

Momentum carried them closer and Scarlett strained to see what it was they were drifting towards. It looked like a figure sitting on a rock. The sobbing was clearly coming from the figure and, as the boat drew closer, Scarlett saw to her amazement that it was a mermaid. The mermaid's hair was the colour of early autumn leaves, and her tail shone as if it were embossed with sapphires and emeralds. Tears ran down the mermaid's cheeks and splashed into the lake below as she pawed at the surface of the lake with her pale hands.

'Hey, are you alright?' Scarlett called, as their boat floated closer, her own heart being wrenched with every sob. The mermaid ignored her, or did not hear, and carried on crying. 'Hey!' Scarlett called again, the distress rising in her voice as their boat came level with the mermaid. Reaching desperately out to her, Scarlett's hand brushed her auburn hair, but their boat was drifting past too quickly. Her tear-streaked face was a mask of absolute sorrow. 'Slow us down! Turn us around!' Scarlett ordered, as she staggered back to her seat. The boat rocked under her careleess steps, threatening to capsize. She took up her oar again and tried to row backwards, but it didn't seem to make any difference. 'Help me out. We have to go back for her!'

Blondie took up an oar as well and they both madly tried to paddle backwards, but the boat kept drifting on at the same speed as if it were simply a ride at a theme park. Scarlett watched the mermaid on her rock shrink and shrink out of sight until she disappeared. It felt as if someone had just punched her in the stomach and left her winded.

'Tilia, who was that?' Scarlett asked, her heart still racing.

'The mermaid of Tears Lake. The story goes that she was, or maybe still is, the most beautiful mermaid in all the worlds. She would sit on her rock in her pond and gaze at her own reflection, singing to herself as mermaids are known to do. Crimsin – through jealousy, or spite or for some dark purpose – took her reflection and cut it away from her. Mermaids' reflections are like our shadows, see. They pin us to our worlds. Since Crimsin took her reflection the mermaid hasn't stopped crying. Her tears flowed and soon the pond became an endless lake. Still, that's how the story goes. No one knows for sure.'

'That's awful,' Scarlett said, a horrible image flashing in her mind of herself, thousands of years from now, roaming Knoware without her shadow, tears streaming down her hollow face – just a story that people barely remembered.

Then Scarlett noticed the shore of the lake all around her again. Behind her, she could see where they had set sail from – the jetty and the wolf's cottage – and could see they were fast approaching the opposite side. The shoreline looked empty of people or animals – just a stony beach that led up to the edge of the forest. Despite this, Scarlett felt as though she were being watched.

'What happened back there?' Scarlett asked, still troubled by the mermaid.

Blondie shrugged her shoulders. 'Weird stuff happens like that here sometimes. You never quite get used to it, though.'

'It was magic,' Tilia said in a serious tone.

'Oh, thank you, Tilia. That clears that up then,' Scarlett said sarcastically and, when the water was shallow enough, she jumped out and pulled the boat onto the shore. Blondie and Tilia jumped onto the gravel shore too and helped to heave the boat out of the water. As Scarlett looked up, she saw, or thought she saw, a flicker of movement from the trees ahead. A dark shape, like a human figure or a grey ghost, seemed to disappear amongst the undergrowth.

Scarlett went to tell the others but then stopped. There was no point worrying them until she knew more or saw it again. Besides, maybe it had just been her imagination.

'Which way, Blondie?' Scarlett asked. Blondie took the map from her pocket and looked around her.

'We have mountains far off to our left and right and, if we've come fairly straight across the lake, we should just carry on north and eventually we'll come to the Luz Mala Marshes. This way then, I guess', and she pointed straight ahead.

They left the stones of the lake shoreline and, after a number of small dunes, headed back into the woods. The forest here felt different to the forest on the other side of the lake, though. It felt older and more claustrophobic, as if the trees here were thicker and older with deeper roots and longer branches. Creepers and vines with purple flowers covered the lower half of all the trees and seemed to shine despite the weak light. Scarlett went over to inspect them having never seen such flowers before in her world.

'Ouch!' Scarlett exclaimed, quickly withdrawing her hand from the vine. A droplet of blood, like a tiny ruby blossomed at the end of her finger. 'Be careful. These vines are covered with tiny thorns,' she said, and popped her bleeding finger into her mouth and carried on walking.

'You have a really great whistle,' Blondie said as they walked carefully between the purple-flowered vines.

'I didn't even notice I was whistling. It's a habit, sorry.'

'No, don't apologise. I mean it. You really do whistle well,' Blondie said sincerely.

'My dad taught me. At least, I think he did. I can't remember really now,' Scarlett said, and pondered why she wasn't more worried about forgetting such big things.

Even though the forest was more foreboding on this side of the lake, she barely heard another sound or saw anything to trouble them until, after a good few hours of walking, they came across a small clearing where they saw a boy and a girl asleep against a tree. The children wore matching blue jumpers and trainers and this, along with their similar ruddy complexions, thin frames and identical curly brown hair, made it clear they were brother and sister.

'Should we wake them?' Blondie asked.

'Erm, hang on a minute,' Scarlett said, and walked over to where they slept, picked up a brown leather satchel that lay next to the sleeping girl and sifted through its contents.

'What are you doing?' Blondie whispered suspiciously, coming over to see what the matter was.

'I was just checking to see if this was my bag. I had one just like it once,' Scarlett said, closing it up. 'My one had different lining, though.'

'Really?' Blondie asked, confused.

'Ok, obviously I wasn't checking to see if it was my bag, Blondie. I was seeing if there was anything worth borrowing.

Not stealing, ok? Just seeing if there were things that we could use on our quest and that I would return in good time.'

'Ahhh!' the boy and girl yelled in unison as they woke up to see the three strangers standing over them. 'Who are you?' the boy asked, with a slight German accent.

'Oh, hi. I'm Scarlett, this is Blondie and Tilia,' Scarlett said, giving them her best smile. Then, even though the light was dim, Scarlett noticed that the two siblings didn't have any shadows. 'Hey, Crimsin took your shadows too!' Scarlett said, excited to find two other children like herself and Blondie. 'We're heading to Crimsin's castle to get our shadows back. Why don't you come with us?' Scarlett asked, holding out her hand to help them stand.

'Go back to Crimsin? Are you crazy?' the girl said, standing up without accepting Scarlett's help.

'We only just escaped from her before. We won't be that lucky again,' the boy said, rising to his feet and brushing himself down.

Scarlett eyed them up and down and crossed her arms tightly in front of her. 'Yeah, you look really lucky, sleeping wild in the woods on your own. You guys really hit the jackpot!'

'Well, at least we're still alive,' the girl replied, not at all intimidated by Scarlett's stern look. 'Which is more than you'll be if you walk into her castle.'

'Don't you want to get home?' Scarlett asked, as the girl picked up her satchel and looked through it suspiciously, clearly noticing it had been moved.

'Of course we do,' the boy said with a sigh. 'It's all we think about – getting back to our father.' He drew little circles with his foot which he stared at intently.

'How did you end up here, then?' Scarlett asked. The girl ignored her and looked away, but her brother seemed eager to talk.

'Our mother wanted us dead. Father was taking us away to the next village where we'd be safe. Only we got separated in the woods. He told us to wait for him, but he couldn't find us again. We searched for him for hours. On our path was a hollow tree trunk. We could have climbed over it but instead we went through it. We came out here and this isn't the same as the wood we were in with father. Something had changed. By the time we realised it, though, we were so lost we couldn't even find the tree trunk again.'

The boy's sister stared at him, her eyes red and wet.

'We could help you find the tree trunk if you like?' Scarlett offered.

'Thanks, but we've already found it again, years ago,' the sister said, wiping her eyes. 'We can't go back through it, though, because she took our shadows. At least, that's what the owl told us.'

'Owl?' Scarlett asked, shaking her head. 'Listen, we're in the same situation. What are your names?' Scarlett asked.

'I'm Hayden and this is my sister Gabrielle,' Hayden said, after looking to his sister to gauge her reaction.

'Gabrielle, come with us,' Scarlett said, genuinely.

'What do you say, sister? Five is safer than two. We could join them. With five of us we might stand a chance of getting our shadows back,' Hayden said, and looked as if he was going to say something else, but then his sister interrupted.

'Thanks, but no thanks,' Gabrielle said, grabbing her brother's arm. 'We're not that stupid!'

Hayden gave an apologetic shrug and allowed himself to be dragged off by his sister into the thicket.

'We left a trail of white pebbles. Look for the white pebbles. Follow them if you get lost,' Hayden's voice called back to them through the undergrowth.

The three of them, resigned to the fact that the siblings weren't coming back, carried on walking, Blondie in the lead with the map, heading north, and Tilia hurrying to keep up.

Every so often on their journey, Scarlett noticed the same dark figure she had seen when she first got off the boat in the trees off to her right. It kept its distance, but now it seemed to be drawing closer ... a shadow in the dark behind the vines with the purple flowers.

'I think we're being followed. There's something dark in the trees over there,' Scarlett said, catching up with Blondie. Blondie just glared at her and carried on walking. 'Didn't you hear me? I said there's something over there in the trees. Some dark shape.' Blondie continued to ignore her. 'Are you angry at me because I was looking in that girl's bag?'

'Yes, Scarlett. You just don't get it, do you?'

'I'm sorry. I do get it. Stealing is wrong.'

'No, you don't, or you wouldn't keep trying to take everything that wasn't nailed down.'

Tilia heard the arguing and came up alongside them.

Scarlett sighed. 'Old habits and all that. I just can't help it. I see something, I just take it. It's a reflex action.'

'That's not an excuse, Scarlett. You have to change,' Blondie said.

'She's right, Scarlett. You must change', and here Tilia walked in front of Scarlett and took her hands in hers. Then, with a look of great reverence and gravity said, 'Just like the caterpillar turns itself into a racoon then into a butterfly, you too can change.'

'What?' Scarlett said, her face screwed into a look of confusion, after giving herself a moment to try to rerun the sentence through her brain to see if she could make sense of it. 'Oh, wait. You mean cocoon, Tilia. Cocoon. And I know have to change. Just give me another chance.'

'What's a cocoon?' Tilia asked.

'It's a little shell the caterpillar makes around itself.'

'So, it can't turn into a ... like ... a big rodent thing – a racoon?'

'No, Tilia,' Scarlett replied, trying not to sound patronising.

'That does make more sense actually. But anyway. If you really do want to change, then we'll help you. Knoware is a good place to change,' Tilia said with a smile. Scarlett thanked them and nodded lots just as if she was back in detention at school. She would change, she told herself. She really would. At least try, anyway.

Following the trails when they could, or cutting off through the trees if Blondie felt the path was leading them anywhere but north, they trudged on. The trees were much further apart here and there was very little undergrowth now – the forest floor was mostly pine needles and dirt and even the vines with the purple flowers seemed fewer in number. Scarlett zipped up her jacket and pulled her hood up as the sun sank lower in the sky.

'What were you like in our world, Blondie? You said you weren't popular. Why?' Scarlett asked as they walked.

Blondie shrugged. 'Can't really remember much anymore. Kids are nasty. They don't need a reason to be mean, do they?'

'I'm sorry. I can't imagine what it's like not to remember your life before,' Scarlett said, not sure if she should put a comforting hand on her back or not.

'Try,' Blondie said.

'Try what? To imagine what it's like for you?'

'No, try and remember your life before. Think of something from your past.'

'Like what?'

'Your bedroom. What did your bedroom look like?

'At my mum's house? Grey carpet, tv, white wardrobe, red-and-white check curtains, a white desk,' Scarlett reeled off, trying to picture it.

'Red-and-white check curtains? You sure?' Blondie asked, squinting at her, as if she didn't quite believe it.

'Yes,' Scarlett said, looking over to her. Then her face dropped. 'No. No, they're not. They're grey too. I think.'

'See!' Blondie said, shrugging her shoulders. 'Your memory of your old life just starts to disappear in this place without your shadow.'

'Blondie, I have to get back, I have to!' she said, grabbing Blondie's shoulders and shaking her.

'I know, I know. That's the plan isn't it?' Blondie said, bringing Scarlett's hands down gently.

'Shhh,' Tilia called from up ahead where she had walked on. 'You hear that?'

The two girls fell silent for a moment and listened. There was a faint rustling sound that could have been any woodland animal.

'I don't hear ... ' but then Scarlett did hear something. A soft, breathing sound that stood out from the rustle of the wind. 'I heard it. I've seen a dark shape following us for miles, but.'

'No. I've seen the dark figure too. It's followed us a long way, since we got off the lake, but I don't think it's that. I heard that panting from the opposite side I saw the dark figure on,' Tilia said, picking up a stout looking stick. Scarlett and Blondie quickly followed suit and picked up sturdy sticks of their own.

Now the breathing sound came from every direction and that's when Scarlett saw the eyes. A set of eyes glowing off in the bushes, reflecting the last of the evening light. She gasped and stepped back, crashing into Blondie who was backing into her. Emerging from the bushes came a wolf. Not like the wolf back in the boat, not like any of the humanoid animals from the village, just a very real, four-legged wolf. A rustle of twigs drew their attention back behind them as another wolf appeared, yellow eyed, staring at the three of them, its tongue lolling between great teeth.

'We're not talking our way out of this one,' Tilia said, backing up next to Scarlett and Blondie to form a tight huddle, all looking outwards. Two other wolves emerged from the undergrowth and surrounded them. Scarlett knew there was no chance in running. Four legs always beat two legs in a race and she doubted she'd even get five paces before she was brought down, the wolf's mouth clamping around her head, its teeth sinking into her neck. One of the wolves raised its head upward to the darkening sky and howled. Scarlett instinctively dropped her stick and threw her hands up to her ears to block out the dreadful sound. It wasn't a lonesome howl that she had heard on films and documentaries. This was a victory cry, the bugle blast before the charge. Dropping their front shoulders, tails raised, the wolves prepared to pounce. Then a woman's shadow walked in front of Scarlett. It casually walked out from the woods and stood straight in front of them. It was as if the person were invisible, but their shadow could still be seen. It was the shadow of a large woman and it stood with its hand on its hips, staring at the largest of the wolves.

The wolves had all seen it too and shuffled backwards, unsure what to make of the creature-less shadow. But the wolves looked hungry and now they had trapped their prey, they didn't look likely to give up. They were still poised to attack, but now their tails had dropped, uncertainty creeping into their stances.

The largest of the wolves, which had a black line of fur running from its nose back over its grey pelt, snarled, baring its teeth, its mouth dripping with saliva. It leapt forward. Instinctively Scarlett ducked and covered her head, but no slashing claws knocked her off her feet and no jaws clamped around her head. Instead, she heard a surprised whimpering cry. She looked up and saw that the shadow of the woman in front of them had caught hold of the wolf's shadow. It pulled the wolf away from the girls by its shadow's tail. The wolf was in such shock that it skipped away some distance before it was brave enough to turn back.

Undeterred, the other wolves remained, but now all their attention was locked onto the shadow. One of the wolves darted forward and bit and snarled and dug at the ground where the shadow was and darted back again, repeating the process several times. The shadow seemed totally unaffected, though, and let the wolf snarl and snap and then slapped the wolf's shadow around the face. Reeling back, the wolf let out a startled yelp and cried out as it ran off into the woods and the other wolves went bounding after it, howling their fears to the setting sun.

Sinking to the ground, Scarlett let out a sigh and began to cry. Blondie was sobbing too. Only Tilia didn't seem traumatised.

'I think we could have taken 'em,' Tilia said, nodding to herself and looking at the patch of trees where the wolves had disappeared from sight. 'I was just getting a spell ready, actually.'

Scarlett laughed despite herself and allowed Tilia to pull her up. In her relief, Scarlett had forgotten about their saviour. She looked over to the woman's shadow. Where the sun was low, the shadow was drawn long and thin and was fading into the gloom around it, but they could all see that the shadow was now waving for them to follow. They looked at each other and shrugged. Scarlett followed the shadow off into the woods.

8

The Old Lady's Shadow

THEY DIDN'T WALK FAR, FIFTEEN MINUTES at the most, before Scarlett spotted a light coming from the trees up ahead. It was a campfire in a small clearing. The pine trees were lit in a soft, flickering glow. In the minutes leading up to this, the fading light had meant that the woman's shadow had almost disappeared into the twilight, merging with the dark. As they approached the fire, though, the woman's shadow suddenly burned back into focus with renewed clarity and it beckoned for them to come forward and sit with her by the fire. The fire was surrounded by four logs and there was a small picnic hamper to one side. Scarlett took up a seat on one side of the shadow, and Tilia sat down on the other. Only Blondie remained standing, her arms folded across her chest.

'This could all be a trap. You know that, don't you?' Blondie said, pacing up and down. The shadow shook its head in reply and beckoned Blondie to go towards the basket. After hesitating a moment, Blondie walked over and, using her foot, carefully lifted the lid as if something might jump out at her.

'What's inside?' Scarlett asked, looking over.

'It looks like bread, cake and fruit,' Blondie said, nudging the side of the basket with her foot to see if anything was hiding underneath.

'I think if the shadow had wanted us dead, it would have just let the wolves eat us,' Tilia said.

'Maybe. But whose shadow is it? It could be Crimsin's for all we know!'

'That's a good point. But I'm starving, so I'm willing to take the risk, especially as it just saved my life! I'll ask the mirror, though, and see what it says if that makes you happier.' She didn't wait for Blondie to reply and pulled the mirror out of her backpack. Looking at the cracked side she asked, 'Can I trust this shadow?'

'Listen to what you're asking? Should you trust a creepy shadow in the middle of the woods that wants to lure you off and feed you food that looks and smells too good to be true? Seriously?' her cracked reflection replied.

'Fair point,' Scarlett said to herself as she turned the looking glass around.

Her unblemished reflection spoke with dazzlingly white teeth, 'The shadow saved your life. Friends come in different forms, Scarlett.'

Scarlett screwed up her lips and nodded thoughtfully. Again, the mirror hadn't told her anything she didn't think already, it was her reflection after all, but it was still good to talk out loud to herself.

'Even if the food is poisoned and we don't eat it, the shadow could still kill us all in our sleep. I say we eat!' Scarlett decided, and she and Tilia got up and grabbed as much as they could carry back to their logs. Armfuls of fruit loaf, blackberries and shiny, red apples. Scarlett stuffed whatever she could fit into her mouth, not realising how hungry she had been. Blondie resisted for a while and then her hunger got the better of her and she began to join in the feast, hardly swallowing what she had in her mouth, before cramming in more food.

After they had eaten most of the contents of the basket, Scarlett flopped down in the warmth of the fire. With her hands rubbing her belly and a smile on her face, she felt herself growing sleepy. Blondie seemed more relaxed now too and even the thought of the wolves still being out there somewhere didn't seem to bother any of them as much as she thought it should. They drew closer to the fire and Tilia put on another log.

With heavy eyes, Scarlett wished them all a good night and lay down, and she was pretty sure that she was asleep before her head had even rested in the crook of her arm.

The next morning, she sat up and took in her surroundings. Orange embers were all that was left of their fire. There was a pink, dawn light that gave the trees around the clearing a soft, warm hue but it wasn't yet strong enough to cast shadows, so the woman's shadow that had saved them the night before could have been long gone or concealed right next to her for all Scarlett knew. Tilia was snoring away, sleeping on her back like a starfish and Blondie was closer to the edge of the clearing, her back to a tree stump. As Scarlett watched her, Blondie started to stir and sat up, rubbing her eyes. 'Morning,' she yawned. 'I'm glad to see we weren't poisoned then.'

Scarlett smiled back. 'It doesn't seem so.'

'Well, that's a good start,' Blondie said, as she popped the perfect, unblemished rose back into golden hair that made it look as though she had just stepped out of the stylist's, not slept on the forest floor.

'How long have you had that rose in your hair?' Scarlett asked.

'Can't remember. I put it in when I first got here, I think. Years now maybe.'

'And it's never withered or wilted or lost a petal?'

'No. Nothing here does, I don't think. Like I said, time works differently in Knoware.'

They both became aware of a faint movement in front of them and, as the forest brightened, the woman's shadow suddenly became visible. It pointed to the bag and indicated for them to quickly follow.

'Tilia's still asleep. Give us a minute,' Scarlett said. As if in reply, from somewhere far off, came angry howling. Tilia sat up, alert and awake.

'Tilia, let's go,' Scarlett said, as she helped her up and grabbed the basket with the last of the food.

They set off at a good pace after the shadow which became more and more distinct as the sun rose higher in the clear blue of the sky. Only as they passed through densely covered patches of wood, where no light filtered through, did they ever lose the shadow. Scarlett noticed that they seemed to be gently travelling down hill through the forest until they came to a shallow stream surrounded by gently swaying willow trees with bright white knotted pearlwort about their roots. After following the stream for hours, they rested up on some rocks which trapped the midday heat next to the bubbling water. There were sparks of rainbow up and down the river as the sun caught the translucent wings of hundreds of emperor dragonflies that skimmed across the water, turning at impossible angles without ever slowing. Flashes of silver shoals of fish darted through emerald weed beneath the surface of the cool, clear water.

It was the shadow who first decided to shuffle closer to the edge and dip its legs into the water, which it did without a ripple or a splash. Scarlett followed suit, and soon all four of them sat in the sun, dipping their legs in the stream as they ate the remaining apples and crusts of bread.

'I've made a decision,' Scarlett said. 'I've decided we will stay here a for a few days.'

Blondie opened her mouth to object, but then slowly closed it again and began to nod. 'That's the best decision you've made all day. Why don't we spend the week here, or maybe longer?'

'Yes!' Scarlett nodded enthusiastically. 'We could stay here forever,' she said as she watched the flashes of emerald and sapphire light from the dragonflies mix with the sparkling sun dance off the river. The two girls splashed their feet in the stream and looked dreamily at the light show.

'What are you two talking about?' Tilia said, turning to them, her face a mask of confusion. 'What about your shadows? And what about the scissors Crimsin stole from me?'

'What shadows? What scissors?' Scarlett and Blondie chorused.

'What's happening?' Tilia blurted out to the shadow as she

scrambled to stand up. The shadow shrugged its shoulders and mimed for Tilia to pull them up. Tilia nodded and took Scarlett's arm. Scarlett pulled away, too mesmerised by the sunlight which split into a thousand flashing fragments on the water's surface.

'Come on!' Tilia said, straining to pull Scarlett to her feet. She may have been small, but Tilia hauled Scarlett to her feet and then yanked Blondie up by her denim top. 'We're getting out of here,' Tilia said, dragging them both away from the water.

Even when they had gone just a few yards from the stream Scarlett felt as though she was waking up from a nap.

'What happened?' Scarlett asked, rubbing her head.

'You just got yourself enchanted,' Tilia said with a knowing nod as they walked further away.

'See, I knew it! The shadow tricked us into going there,' Blondie spat, pointing accusingly at the shadow. The shadow put its hands up and shook its head.

'I don't think so,' Tilia said. 'I felt no evil there. There are many enchanted and bewitching places in the world. Few are good or evil. They just are. I didn't feel anything there, but then you humans are more susceptible to magic.'

'Maybe. Maybe not. We'll see,' Blondie said as she stared at the shadow through squinted eyes.

Despite Blondie's reservations, Scarlett continued to follow the shadow, cutting further away from the stream. She found her head cleared better if she whistled – it seemed to drown out the confusion. So she whistled 'Run the World' by Beyoncé and, sometime late in the afternoon, when the shadows started to grow longer, a pink cottage came into view which they were evidently heading towards. It was a simple building of black timbers and painted stone and it was surrounded by the most lovingly tended garden with chalky, baby-blue hydrangeas and beds of white cuckoo flowers and daffodils. Scarlett opened the low wooden gate and the four of them walked halfway up the flagstone path and stopped as the shadow slipped inside under the door.

'You still think it could be a trick by Crimsin?' Scarlett asked, turning to Blondie. 'Get off the flowers, geez, look what a mess you've made,' she chastised, as Tilia looked at the trampled flowers beneath her feet and made an apologetic face, stepping back onto the path. Scarlett walked forwards and approached the door not waiting for an answer.

The door had a little square window in the middle, but the curtain was drawn across it so she couldn't see inside. Scarlett was just about to knock when the door opened and there, standing in front of her, was her grandma. At least, that was her first impression, and her second impression too. It was only after a shocked and speechless few moments that Scarlett saw enough differences to make her realise that it wasn't her grandma, but she was so similar in looks and stature that this lady must surely have been her grandmother's sister.

Her short hair, greying gracefully – that warm smile that spread to every corner of her face – her sparking eyes. There was so much that was nearly identical.

'You look exactly like my grandma,' Scarlett blurted out.

'I get that a lot,' the old lady said.

'Hang on!' Blondie said, a look of confusion scrunching up

her face as she pushed next to Scarlett to get a better look. 'She looks exactly like my nan too! She even has the same tattoos! Wait. No, they *are* different.'

'Well, I hatched from a magic egg, but I often picture what my grandmother might have looked like if I'd had one and you are the spitting image of it!' Tilia joined in, squeezing between them.

'How can you look like all our grandmas – real or imagined?' Scarlett asked, pointing at the old lady who laughed a jolly laugh to herself as she walked back into her cottage and made herself comfortable at the end of a sofa by an open fire. It wasn't a mocking or evil laugh, it was an honest, cheerful laugh and the fact that she looked just like her grandma put Scarlett at ease. The three of them edged inside.

'My dear ladies, I am Oma and it is my blessing and my curse to look to others almost exactly like their own grandmothers,' she said, as way of an introduction, pouring out four teas and adding a splash of milk to the china crockery that sat on a delicate little table in front of her. She then picked up a sugar cube, and pinched its shadow with her fingers, plucking the shadow away and tossing it into the corner of the room as if it were something solid and tangible. Oma's shadow, which they had followed to the cottage, had made itself comfy in the shadow of an armchair in the corner of the room, and it caught the shadow of the sugar cube in its hand and ate it. Oma smiled at their astonished faces as she picked up the shadowless sugar cube and dropped it into her own tea.

'They never taste quite as sweet without their shadows,

though. I expect life isn't so sweet either, Scarlett, without yours, is it?'

'Hey, how do you know all this? Is this some trap of Crimsin's?' Scarlett said, backing up to the door again, where she was tightly flanked by Blondie and Tilia.

'No, Scarlett. My shadow has been watching you for a while. What she sees and hears I see and hear. I also have some friends in Hapglade that report back to me. You even stayed in their bed-and-breakfast I believe. See, nothing very sinister or very clever, I assure you.'

Scarlett nodded, 'Fine. I guess that's okay then', and she took a seat on the sofa opposite to Oma. Blondie and Tilia joined her, all sitting rigid and ready to flee at any moment. They stared at Oma, still finding it strange that she looked exactly like their grandmothers. There was a part of Scarlett that just wanted to go over and hug her, but she wasn't quite her gran, and this made her feel very strange at the same time.

'So, how have you been feeling, Scarlett?' Oma asked, after a brief silence.

Scarlett looked thoughtful, turning her head to one side and nibbling her bottom lip. 'I don't feel the same without my shadow. Like, I'm forgetting who I was. As if that part of me is fading away. I can't remember what my house looks like now, or what my dad sounded like. I didn't even remember I had a grandma until I saw you.'

'That's what happens when your shadow gets taken away. Our shadows are what keep us grounded – anchored to the world. Without it, the real you will slowly slip away as it almost has done with your companion,' Oma said, looking over to Blondie.

'Will you help me get my shadow back? And Blondie's?' Scarlett asked, shuffling forwards in her seat, tears welling in her eyes.

'Of course, Scarlett. I will do what I can. Although – '

'How do we know we can trust you?' Blondie interrupted. 'Sorry, but how do we know you never sent the wolves and made it look like you saved us, to trick us into trusting you and coming to the stream or to here? We don't know you're really friends with the three bears,' Blondie said as she took the teacup out of Scarlett's hands before she could take a sip. 'How do we know you haven't poisoned our tea? It smells proper funny.'

'It's called camomile tea and, well, I guess you don't know for sure,' Oma said with an honest smile that started in her twinkling eyes and spread out to a sea of deep wrinkles.

'Well, there is one way actually,' Scarlett said, and sheepishly took the mirror out of her bag. 'Could I ask you to look into this?'

'What have we here?' Oma asked, taking the mirror carefully from Scarlett's hand and examining it. 'Ah-hah!' she said, recognising the object. 'A two-faced mirror. I didn't think there were any of these left in our world. Not anymore. Where did you get it?'

Blondie crossed her arms, tapped her foot and raised an eyebrow. 'Yeah, Scarlett. Where did you get it from?'

'Well, for *your* information, I didn't steal it, Blondie. Mummy Bear gave it to me, if you must know,' Scarlett said with a smile for Blondie's benefit. 'Now, Oma. I just need you to look into it for me.'

Oma lifted the mirror to look into it as Scarlett came around behind her and gasped at what she saw. Oma's reflection was of an ageless woman. If Scarlett had to describe Oma's reflection, one moment she would have said she was dark skinned, with deep brown eyes and then the next moment she would have said the reflection was pale skinned, with emerald eyes and auburn hair, yet somehow her reflection never changed at all either.

'You must help this girl,' Oma's reflection said back to Oma. Oma turned the mirror around and stared at the cracked side. 'You must help this girl,' the same, shifting, yet static, reflection said.

'You see,' Oma said, laying down the mirror carefully on her lap. 'I appear to others as they remember their grandmothers, and so my reflection is made up of every one of those images. Thousands over the years. But I hope that proves that I don't have a darker set of motives. And I intend to take my own advice and help you how I can,' she said, and poured herself more tea. 'The best way I can help you all, is to tell you what you will now face. From here, you still have a long journey ahead of you until the forest turns into swamp land. You will come to a place where marshes spread out as far as the eye can see. Pools of mud that will swallow any traveller and his horse and cart who are foolish enough to wander off the safe path in the Luz Mala Marshes. My shadow can lead you to the edge of this land, but it can't go any further. For a start, there is not light enough to cast a shadow you could see, and secondly, my powers do not stretch beyond my borders. So, through the marshland you must all go without me. Then, after the Luz Mala Marshes you must cross the Giant Plains and only then you will find the town of Bitterfall where Crimsin's castle is – a giant, black-stoned monstrosity that over-shadows the folk of the town below it. The bridge to Crimsin's castle is guarded by wolves, both two legged and four legged. It won't be easy to get past them.'

'Sounds easy to me. I have a spell for that,' Tilia said, leaning back and nodding.

Scarlett rolled her eyes. 'But just in case Tilia happens to forget that spell before we get there, what do you recommend?'

Oma topped up her own tea for a third time. 'In the town of Bitterfall, close to Crimsin's castle, is an inn called The Cruel Crow. Between midnight and sunrise there used to be a certain fox who could be found at the back of the inn selling magical items and important information of dubious acquisition. He's a nice enough fellow, but he can't really be trusted. He might even be dead, for all I know. He certainly had enough enemies. But if there is a way to get in, he'll know it.'

Scarlett nodded in response. 'And so, this fox is just going to hand this information over to us?' Scarlett asked.

'No. Sir Fox never does anything for free, or even for cheap. But you're all resourceful young women. I'm sure you'll figure something out. He likes to make bets, if that's useful information,' Oma said, and turned to look at the clock on the wall behind her which had no hands. 'Goodness, it's getting late, and you won't be travelling any further tonight. I have rooms for the three of you. Then, in the morning, my shadow will lead you to the edge of the Luz Mala Marshes.'

Oma moved the table a little away from her and pushed herself up. 'Your rooms are made up especially for you,' she said, making her way across the thick floral rugs. 'This is your room, Blondie.'

Blondie walked over and stopped in the doorway to her room, reaching out a hand to steady herself. 'I remember this room,' she said, and Scarlett came up alongside her.

The bedroom was completely out of place in the quaint cottage. Scarlett had expected it to be full of old wooden furniture and china ornaments, but it wasn't. It was magenta pink and covered in posters of singers and bands she didn't recognise with names like 'Roxette' and 'Blur' and one poster was of a very young Will Smith that said 'The Fresh Prince'. There was a poster for a film called *Robin Hood: Prince of Thieves* and Scarlett wondered if the person who had put up so many posters was trying to cover up as much of the hideous pink as possible. A silver television – one of those ones that had a tiny screen, but an enormous back and was the shape of a cube, sat on something that looked like a giant DVD player, only it had a huge slot at the front that could have fitted a fat book inside it.

'I remember this! This is my room – my room from home,' Blondie said, stepping inside and taking it all in. She went up and touched the posters. As Blondie opened the door to her wardrobe, Scarlett could see it was plastered with photos of Blondie with different friends. One of her and a small group all sticking their tongues out on a coach trip, Blondie and a friend in a park somewhere. 'How? How have you done this?'

'I don't make the rooms. They are made up for you. It's only what is in your head. Even if you can't remember it,' Oma explained.

'I couldn't. I couldn't remember it, not until I saw it here. Now it's all come back to me,' Blondie said, running her fingers lightly over the photos.

'And this is your room, Scarlett,' Oma said, leading Scarlett out of Blondie's bedroom to the room next door. Scarlett took hold of the door handle, paused, and then pushed it open. It was her bedroom from her mum's house. There was her flat-screen television mounted on the cream wall, her grey carpet, her white Ikea wardrobe that she had insisted on. Her matching white desk with her laptop closed. It felt as if she hadn't seen her room in years.

'Sleep tight,' Oma called from outside as she led Tilia further down the corridor.

Scarlett closed her bedroom door and looked around. She was back. Back in her own room. But when she lifted the blind, there was Oma's garden, silhouettes of flowers bobbing in the evening breeze.

She sat on her bed and lifted her duvet to her face, and it smelled of home. Lying down, she pulled the duvet tightly around her, scrunching fistfuls of it to her face. The familiar fabric softener transported her to a lazy afternoon when she listened to Taylor Swift on repeat and the sun shone and she didn't have a care in the world. Then the tears came as all her memories came back – things she didn't even know she had forgotten. The time when Scarlett couldn't stop laughing until her throat throbbed and burned. It was last Christmas dinner and her mum had sneeze-farted at the table as she was taking a drink. In the summer holidays just past when she and her dad had swum out to sea and she had got cramp and her dad had put her on his shoulders and walked back to shore having swallowed a gallon of salt water. Memories that made her who she was. Memories she would lose forever if she didn't get her shadow back.

After her sobbing slowed, Scarlett drifted off to sleep, swimming through her past.

Opening her eyes as the morning rays lit the room through the blinds, she wondered for a moment if she had woken up back in the real world, in her bedroom at her mum's and Knoware had all been a dream. But she could feel she wasn't home. It looked like her room; it had even felt like her room last night. But today the room had a plastic feel to it. Like a waxwork copy of her room.

As she knew they would be, it was Blondie and Tilia who were making breakfast at the table outside her bedroom, not her mum on the landing. It had been no dream, at least not one she had woken up from yet. But she knew more than ever what she had to do now. She would find Crimsin, and get her shadow back. No. Not just hers. Everyone's. Everyone's shadow and reflection and the scissors and whatever else Crimsin had stolen.

'Morning. Did you sleep well?' Oma asked, as she walked in from the kitchen carrying a tea tray. Scarlett nodded, a defiant smile on her face.

They all breakfasted with little conversation. Sleeping in her own bedroom had made her realise how much she had forgotten already and how much she missed home and, by the look on Blondie's face, Scarlett thought she must have felt the same way too. Except, it would have been a thousand times worse for Blondie because she had nearly forgotten all about her life before. To be reminded of everything so suddenly and in such startling detail must have been almost too much to take.

'What was your room like?' Scarlett asked Tilia, when she had finished her cup of tea.

'Can you imagine seeing your own soul reflected in a pearl at the bottom of a stream?' Tilia asked.

'Not really,' Scarlett admitted.

'Well, it was a bit like that anyway.'

Scarlett nodded and ate the last of her toast. 'Cool.'

When the breakfast bits had been cleared away, Scarlett and the others congregated at the front door with all their stuff. 'Thank you, Oma, for everything you've done for us,' Scarlett said, and squeezed her tight. Oma even smelled like her nan – lemon and ginger.

Oma hugged them all, handed out cake and fruit wrapped in a red and white polka-dot handkerchief and blew them a kiss from her front door.

'Stick to the paths. Trust in each other!' Oma called out from her cottage as her shadow led them further into the forest.

9

The Luz Mala Marshes

IN THE DAPPLED MORNING LIGHT, SCARLETT and her two companions followed Oma's shadow through the young pines with their dew-covered, fragrant needles. Birds tweeted excitedly in the canopy above them as they travelled below.

'Okay, so what did you steal from her?' Blondie asked when they had walked for a few minutes, Oma's shadow leading without hesitation when the path forked.

'Blondie! I'm offended. Even I wouldn't steal from my own gran!' Scarlett said, genuinely taken aback.

Blondie sighed. 'I'm sorry. That was mean.'

'It's okay. Don't worry about it. To tell you the truth, there was nothing worth nicking. Her drawers were just full of costume jewellery and hankies,' Scarlett said, not looking around, although she could feel Blondie's stare, trying to work out if she was joking or not.

They carried on following Oma's shadow as it led them through the forest and, as the day grew on, the trees became thinner and sicklier looking. Mud began to squelch over Scarlett's red Converse trainers and the sweet, pine smell of the woods was replaced with the rancid odour of decaying plants. The tweeting of birds changed to the cawing of crows.

When they stopped to eat lunch, it was difficult to find dry ground. By dinner time, finding footing that didn't end with Scarlett sinking up to her knees in mud became increasingly difficult, and when the sunlight grew dim, Scarlett suddenly realised that they would no longer be able to see Oma's shadow.

'Quick, we need to get as far as we can! The light's fading,' she shouted to the others as they pressed on. As frantic as Scarlett was, the thick mud made going quickly impossible, and as the mud began to rise around her legs, Oma's shadow stopped walking and turned to her. The shadow waved goodbye as it became fainter and hard to distinguish in the gloom. Then, as a low ceiling of dark clouds rolled over the weak sun, Oma's shadow disappeared completely. Scarlett felt her heart sink. They had lost their guide and lost a powerful friend and now night was setting in and the mud was turning to swampland. They were at the edge of the Luz Mala Marshes and she felt exposed and vulnerable.

They walked on in silence as a fog rose from the marshes around them and merged with the low-hanging, grey clouds above. The oppressive greyness was disheartening, and it meant that they could no longer tell which way they were walking with the sun completely hidden. It was impossible to even tell in which quarter of the sky the sun might be hiding.

'You sure we're still going the right way?' Scarlett asked, her voice seeming to bounce about in the fog like a lost echo.

'Not really. I hope so. This place gives me the creeps,' Blondie said, looking around.

Scarlett nodded. 'I agree.' All around her, skeletal trees hung on to life in the marshy ground. A thin veil of damp mist clung to everything and made seeing any further than a stone's throw away almost impossible. Strange flickers of green light caught the corners of their eyes, but when they looked around there was nothing there.

The three of them paused as the path they were on split three ways and each vein of path narrowed to thin strips of solid earth. Each one ran on for fifty or so yards and split again. Scarlett knew that following the wrong path could lead them to dead ends or tracking back or an untimely death.

'We could be here for days. Forever!' Blondie said, trying to choose which of the paths looked best.

Tilia stepped up and tested the centre path with her foot. 'Your guess is as good as mine, but I'd go for the middle one if I had to choose. Looks more solid.'

'Hey, wait. Look at that,' Scarlett said, and pointed to something on the track to the right. It was a pale, white pebble and it stuck out amongst the brownish mud like a beacon. 'This was what Hayden was talking about. He said they had left a trail. We just have to follow the white pebbles!'

Finding the trail of white pebbles lifted Scarlett's spirits immediately. In fact, it made the next few hours almost fun, spotting the pebbles and following the path, sure that they were heading the right way and that they would be out of the mire soon. But the scant light they were working by was fading fast.

They had only just seen and found the last white pebble without falling off the path. Scarlett knew that it would have been foolish to wander on much further with so little light and so much danger.

'We should stop for the night,' Blondie said, as if reading her mind.

'Agreed, although I doubt I'll sleep much here,' Scarlett said. 'I'm glad I got a good night's sleep at Oma's.'

They found a patch of dry land that they could all sit on back to back and they ate some of the cake that Oma had given them. They tried to get as comfy as they could and Scarlett took the mirror from her backpack, which she laid in front of her. The other two wouldn't stop fidgeting and strange slurping, bubbling sounds rose from the mud around her as if things moved just below the surface. Occasionally they would all jump just as they were nodding off when they heard, or thought they heard, something or someone cry out and then fall suddenly silent. The strange, ghostly green lights continued to flare for a second and then disappear and not come back when they stared at them. And if the fidgeting, the ghost lights and the strange noises weren't going to prevent her from sleeping, the cold was. Her legs were caked in cold mud and her fingers were numb. She pulled her red hood tightly around her head and closed her eyes, just to rest them, and leant her head on Tilia's and Blondie's shoulders and somehow she drifted off into an uncomfortable doze.

Scarlett woke with a start, as if she had been falling in a dream and woken at the moment she was about to hit the floor. Her neck ached from sleeping in a strange position and her clothes were damp and cold. It took a few seconds to bend and stretch her legs into life before she was able to stand. She wasn't sure if it was even morning yet. She guessed it was as the sky was now light grey rather than dark grey. Putting the mirror back in her backpack, she was ready to wake the others up and get moving again but then she was suddenly hit with a wave of terrible despair. If Knoware was draining her memory, then the Luz Mala Marshes were sapping her hope. The endless bleakness, the cold – it sank into her bones leaving no room for optimism or courage.

Before waking the others, she looked around to find the next stone, trying to remember which way they had been heading, trying to remember what the whole point of this journey was. That was when the gold caught her eye.

Just off the path, on another thin ridge of dry land, gleamed a golden coin. It was gleaming so brightly; it was as if a ray of sun was shining on it alone in that colourless land. A little bit of hope, a little bit of happiness in that marshland of despair. Scarlett looked back at her companions; they were still fast asleep. She was about to wake them and tell them to come with her, but she hesitated. They'd try and stop her, or Blondie would want the coin, she just knew it. The others would make her share it. And she would share it, of course she would. But just in case she didn't want to, she'd just go and get it herself. It would only be a quick jump there and back. A little gold coin would make her happy, would brighten the morning.

Then again, if she fell back, or didn't jump far enough, she would sink below the mud with a scream that would be lost below the mire. But the coin winked at her. It looked so beautiful, so golden. She would do it. She needed it.

Walking to the edge of her island of dry land, she estimated the jump. Then she took a few steps back and ran, leaping into the air and making the jump with ease. She ran over and picked up the coin. Easy, she thought, looking back to the others still asleep. Looking around her before she headed back, she noticed another flash of gold just a little way down this new path. It was barely twenty steps away. It would be silly to make the jump for one coin when she could just walk a little further and get two.

She pulled the second coin out from the mud where it was half buried and put in into her jacket pocket with the other one and there, just a couple of little dirt islands away, were two more coins. She made these two jumps without hesitation, striding from one to the other. Putting the coins into her pocket again, she saw another coin on a large island of land where the bare and black remains of what must once have been a huge, proud tree sat.

Hopping to it, she picked up the coin that was caught between two tree roots, certain in her mind that she would make this the last one. Looking back to see if the others were awake, though, she realised that she could no longer see them through the fog. It didn't matter, though. She could easily retrace her steps. She just had to hop back across the two little islands – only she could no longer see them either. Twice she must have walked full circle around the tiny island, but there were no solid mounds of earth to jump to. Her heart started to beat faster as she realised how stupid she'd been.

'Blondie!' she called in the direction she thought they were. Only silence came back to her through the fog. Then came a low creaking sound from somewhere on the island. She looked about her. There was nowhere to hide. Nothing else was there apart from her and the dead tree. The creaking came again, and this time Scarlett caught movement in the corner of her eye. It looked as though something dark had moved amongst the tree roots. She stared and realised with horror as the creaking came again, that it wasn't something in the tree roots that was moving at all. It was the tree roots themselves. They shot towards her like angry, writhing snakes and coiled about her body. She cried out, but they constricted around her chest, making it difficult to breathe. Effortlessly, the roots pulled her over and drew her towards the tree that was opening; a giant cleft in its trunk widening like a vertical mouth. In the seconds before she passed out, Scarlett saw herself being pulled inside and felt as if she were being drawn down into the cold earth.

10

Beneath the Tree

THE FIRST THING SCARLETT SAW WHEN she woke up, was eerie green flames from the torches on the walls of what looked like a mud cave. She struggled to sit up, her body bruised and aching. She remembered being dragged into the tree and down into the ground, but that seemed like a lifetime ago. She was relieved to find she still wore the backpack and then she saw Blondie and Tilia sitting at her feet.

'Hey, I thought I'd lost you both,' Scarlett laughed, a great rush of joy washing over her. Then she noticed the cage. A cage seemingly made out of the ribs of some giant animal. 'Where are we?'

'We don't know. But we do know that we're now the prisoners of Rancan,' Blondie said, wiping her red eyes, and it was clear that she'd been crying.

'Who's Rancan?' Scarlett asked with a gulp.

'I'm Rancan,' came a harsh, raspy voice from the other end of the mud cave. 'Lord of the Marshes and owner of any meat that strays from the safe path.'

Scarlett gasped as she saw Rancan waddle forwards, all six foot and twenty stone of him. He had the body of a giant frog – pale and flabby with long back legs and podgy webbed hands. Only he didn't have the head of a frog – his head was that of a vulture. His neck was a long scrawny bend on the end of which sat a giant, bald, beaked head with two fearsome yellow eyes. 'So lonely in the Luz Mala Marshes. So lonely. Now more friends come,' Rancan continued as he waddled closer, stepping over what Scarlett guessed were the bones of former guests.

Scarlett pushed herself back into the corner as far as she could as Rancan, holding a green flamed torch in one hand, came over to inspect his new visitors.

'I keep you here, I will. All friends. All friends. We have nice chats, every day,' Rancan squawked.

'Please, please let us go. You have to let us go. You can't keep us here,' Scarlett pleaded, feeling her whole body begin to shake.

'I like to eat rat eggs ... ' Rancan said, ignoring her completely.

'Please, we need to get our shadows back,' Blondie joined in, pressing her face against the rib-cage.

' ... and I like drinking frog milk,' Rancan continued, much the same way a budgie keeps squawking away to itself no matter what you say.

'Let us go and we promise to ... ' but Scarlett didn't know what she could promise him.

'I do like the smell of sticks,' Rancan cawed on, going from one inane subject to the next. Scarlett tried to beg and plead, but Rancan was pitiless in his rambling. Never once did he acknowledge what they said in return. Scarlett gave up talking and covered her face with her hands and cried.

Hours went by with his unrelenting gibberish until finally he started to yawn and wandered off.

'Scarlett, what are we going to do?' Blondie asked.

Scarlett shook her head, her eyes red and puffy. 'I don't know. Tilia, do you have a spell to get us out?' she asked, with no real hope.

'As a matter of fact, I do actually,' Tilia replied.

Scarlett frowned. 'You do. Like, seriously you have a spell to get us out?'

Tilia nodded. 'I just need a few last ingredients for my spell.'

Scarlett sat up straighter, giving Tilia her full attention. 'Okay, what is it that you need?' she asked, thinking what things she had in her pockets and her bag.

'To finish off my magic spell, I just need a lockpick, a hacksaw and some dynamite,' Tilia said with a straight face.

Scarlett sank against the wall again. 'Good night, Tilia.'

That night, Scarlett felt awful. They were trapped in some dank and muddy prison all because she wanted a few sparkly coins. She felt them in her pocket and they were cold and greasy. What was worse was that Blondie had barely said two words to her. She knew, Scarlett thought. Blondie knew that Scarlett had wandered off and left them to look for gold and now Blondie would never forgive or trust her again. Scarlett went to say something to her but then stopped. What could she say? What words made up for the fact that her greed had got them trapped forever. She didn't sleep much at all that night. She just lay there, watching the light of the green flames flicker on the ceiling making the shapes of wolves and fat frogs and vultures.

Sometime later – it could have been morning, it could have been evening, with only the glow of the green lamps, it was impossible to tell – Rancan returned.

'I'm Rancan,' came the familiar, parrot-like voice. 'Lord of the Marshes and owner of any meat that strays from the safe path.' He waddled up to the cage, and to Scarlett he looked as though he were grinning, but she wasn't sure that beaks could grin.

'How many sticks make a pile?' he cawed loudly to Scarlett and the others. 'Yes, a big pile of sticks,' he replied to some imagined answer in its head.

'Please, Rancan, let us go!' Scarlett begged, already exhausted at the thought of another day of being spoken at.

'Dry mud is good for standing! Wet mud is good for sitting!' Rancan cried.

'You're not listening!' Scarlett shouted, losing her temper, tears welling in her eyes again. 'You're just talking away to yourself,' she sobbed and immediately stopped, a plan popping into her head. 'You like talking away to yourself, right?' Scarlett said, turning around and rummaging through her bag until she found what she was looking for. She pulled out the mirror so that Rancan could see his reflection.'

'Green mud is nice!' Rancan screeched at his reflection in the mirror.

'Brown mud is nice!' the reflection said back to him and Rancan squawked with delight.

'Boiled rat eggs for tea!'

'Boiled rat eggs for breakfast!' his reflection said. On and on Rancan went, chatting away to his reflection who chatted back to him, neither of whom really listened to what the other was saying, just waiting for their turn to speak, but perfectly content talking away to something else.

Scarlett lowered the mirror.

'Hey, bring me back!' Rancan cried out, his yellow eyes narrowing, his sharp beak snapping hungrily to itself. It was the first time he had reacted to anything she had done or said. His breath carried to her and smelt of rot and decay.

'I will. You can keep this mirror, but only if you let us go,' Scarlett demanded.

'No. Guests must stay,' Rancan said, shaking his giant head backwards and forwards.

'Then the mirror goes away. Or maybe I'll even break it!' Scarlett said, raising it above her head.

'No. No. You go. You go. Me stay. Me in the glass stay,' Rancan said. He waddled over to the wall, his flat webbed feet slapping on the wet floor, and pulled a wooden lever underneath a green-flamed torch on the wall with his flabby hands. With a rumble, the bone bars opened like the jaws of some giant shark, and Scarlett and the others darted free. Scarlett grabbed her bag, tossing the mirror to Rancan as they ran past him up some crudely carved stone steps and out into the middle of the marshes.

They left the sound of Rancan chatting away to himself down in the cave as they followed the single path away from his prison. Scarlett was worried that they would soon get lost again but, although the path from Rancan's lair was winding, it seemed to be leading them out of the Luz Mala Marshes. The sky was brightening and the mist thinning out.

'What happened back there? Did you wander off without us?' Blondie asked stiffly, after they were well clear of the cave.

'I thought I heard someone in trouble,' Scarlett lied. 'I just went to see if I could see anyone.'

'Yeah?' Blondie asked. 'Nothing to do with that clinking sound coming from your pockets then?'

'Fine, look, I mucked up, okay? I got greedy and went off looking for coins.' She took them out of her pockets and saw that they weren't golden at all. They were just iron coins, and quite small at that. 'They looked more impressive earlier. The marshes were just getting me down. I don't know. It was kind of like the river and the dragon flies, maybe I was just a little enchanted. I just felt I needed the coins to be happy. Maybe we'll still be able to use them somehow?' she said, trying to sound cheery, as if being caught by a giant frog vulture might have been worth the terror all along. Blondie simply stared at her then turned away. The air was definitely becoming warmer and less foul.

'Well, it's a shame we didn't have any dynamite for my spell,' Tilia said, almost to herself. Scarlett and Blondie ignored her.

'I have to hand it to you, though, Scarlett. You always seem to come up smelling of roses,' Blondie said, then seemed to grimace and spat something into her hand. 'Errgh!'

'What's wrong?' Scarlett asked, hurrying over to her. In a little pool of saliva in Blondie's hand, sat a white, chewed up ball of gum.

'My gum! It just lost all its flavour,' Blondie said, staring at the gum as if it couldn't be real. 'You said I've been here twenty-eight years. I've had that gum twenty-eight years and it's never lost its flavour! I don't get it? Why now?'

'Look at your rose too,' Scarlett said, and took the rose carefully from Blondie's hair. Even as she took it, petals came loose and fluttered to the floor. All three huddled around the rose, not the bright, cherry-red rose it had been the day before, but now a dark maroon colour, like an old blood stain.

'What does this mean?' Blondie asked.

'Maybe it's because we crossed the swamp?' Scarlett said looking back the way they had come. 'Is that possible, Tilia, because we've crossed the marshes? Does that mean we will start to get older now too?'

Tilia shook her head, which turned into nodding, then she shrugged. 'Magic's complicated.'

'That's not helpful, Tilia!' Scarlett said. 'Will we start aging now?'

'Probably. But I don't know how magic affects humans here. It's very different for us magical people. Crossing the swamps might mean that whatever magic stopped you from changing back there doesn't apply here,' Tilia admitted.

'That means, if Crimsin imprisons us here, we're slowly going to get older and die?'

'Yes, maybe so. And the older you get, the less likely it is that your shadow will still fit you. If we don't get your shadows back to you both soon, they may never fit again, and then you'll both be here forever!'

11

Crossing the Giant Plains

THE SWAMP FOG FROM THE LUZ Mala Marshes thinned out further and then, in what seemed like only a few steps, it cleared completely. Blue skies soared above Scarlett and she felt the warmth of the sun on her face and, with it, hope seemed to return.

'Wow, we're nearly there. I can see Crimsin's castle in the distance!' Blondie said, pointing ahead over the plains.

Scarlett saw that she was right. The grassy plain they found themselves on stretched to the horizon without hill or rise for miles, but there, in the distance, could clearly be seen the small town of Bitterfall with a large, black castle behind it. Bright yellow buttercups and dandelions were dotted all over the plains, along with a few other flowering weeds, but apart from that, the plains were featureless. There was no bird sound, but the wind moved through the long grasses and brought with it the scent of spring. The sky was a rich blue with little wisps of white clouds scudding across it. Only at the skyline did the clouds darken and seem to gather together, creating a grey mountain to frame Crimsin's castle. It looked like storm clouds were gathering far off in the distance, but Scarlett didn't let it get her down.

'When Oma said that these were called the Giant Plains,' she said to her companions, 'I thought they would be huge, and we'd be travelling them for days or weeks. But we can see the castle, Tilia!' Scarlett said, pleased her journey had reached the final stretch.

'No. That's not why they're called the Giant Plains,' Tilia laughed. 'They're called the Giant Plains because giants live here.'

'I'm sorry?' Scarlett said, not sure if she had heard Tilia correctly.

'No need to be sorry. You didn't put them here,' Tilia said seriously. 'Don't know how they got here. But we don't want to run into one. They tend to eat anything that moves. You won't find another animal on these plains, not unless it wandered here by mistake, and then it won't last long. All gobbled up it will be,' Tilia said cheerily.

'And when did you plan on telling us this?' Scarlett asked, accusingly. 'Just before or after we were eaten?'

'Oh, before, I guess,' Tilia replied.

Even this fact couldn't dampen Scarlett's spirits, though. As horrible as the giants sounded, the ground was flat and dry from here to Bitterfall and, without a hill or tree in sight, she couldn't see where a giant could possibly be hiding. They would surely be able to spot one a mile or so off and that would give them plenty of time to lie low or run or think of something.

'Well, should we wait for night to try to make it across? We'll be harder to see for any giant, but then we won't be able to spot them so easily ourselves,' Scarlett asked.

'I'd rather see what was coming than stumble about in the dark,' Blondie said. They both looked to Tilia. 'What do you think?'

'Sooner the better,' Tilia agreed.

'Right, let's go,' Scarlett said, and they began to stride off over the green plains under a blue sky towards the darkening patch of clouds and the town of Bitterfall that sat before it.

Blondie seemed to have forgiven, or at least forgotten, Scarlett's wandering off in the Luz Mala Marshes, Tilia was humming to herself, and with the sun on her face, Scarlett hadn't felt this positive about her journey since she had first set off with Blondie from the three bears' house. She began to whistle an old Taylor Swift song to herself, bright and tuneful and she was just thinking what a lovely whistle she had – when a giant sat up next to her.

Scarlett jumped a foot in the air and clutched her heart as the man mountain rose up from the hole he had been lying in, completely hidden from view.

'Chee, chi, cho, churl, I smell the blood of an English girl!' the giant bellowed, then yawned and stretched, showing off a mouthful of rotten, crooked teeth. He was twenty or so feet high, and he was still sitting down. His head was the size of a garden shed and covered in coarse black hair and he was looking about his crater for the source of the smell. He had all the features of a man, just a very ugly one. His forehead stuck out above his eyes, he barely had a chin and he had big, black bags under his eyes.

The giant was in a massive crater in the ground unadorned with any furniture or luxury. There were a few utensils, like a large knife, a cooking pot and long club, but nothing to lie on or sit in.

'Oooo! Lunch,' he said, standing up to his full height as he saw them.

I could run, Scarlett thought. If we all ran in different directions maybe he wouldn't get us all, but he would get at least one of us. The other two both looked to Scarlett as the giant climbed out of his pit and stood over them. Scarlett didn't even come up to the top of his knees.

'Wait. You can eat me and my friend, but you can't eat our genie,' Scarlett said, and both Tilia and Blondie stared at her. 'Just go with me!' Scarlett whispered to them.

'Genie? What, this one?' he said, pointing a massive log of a finger at Tilia. 'Doesn't look much like a genie.'

'Oh, it is. Very powerful. We're taking it to Crimsin so it can grant her three wishes.'

'I am?' Tilia asked, her face wrinkled in confusion.

'You are. And we just hope that no one gets to her before Crimsin does and steals the three wishes for themselves,' Scarlett continued.

'What? So, this one here can grant three wishes?'

'Yes.'

'So, what's to stop me stealing her and taking the three wishes for myself?' the giant asked.

'Well, nothing apart from eating us, I guess,' Scarlett admitted.

The giant frowned. 'Why can't I eat you two?'

'We help her grant the wishes, obviously. Without us, the magic doesn't work,' Scarlett said, as if it should have been clear.

The giant scratched his head and looked very thoughtful for a good long while. 'Okay, so who was the genie?'

'This one! Goodness me. Let me make this easy for you. You say,' and here Scarlett deepened her voice, 'I'm stealing the wishes. For my first wish I want diamonds and gold and treasure.'

'Why would I want diamonds and gold and treasure?' the giant asked.

'So, you could be rich!'

'Why do I want to be rich?'

'So you can spend the whole day sleeping and doing what you want.'

'That's what I do now.'

'Okay. Good point. Fine, not rich then. What's your name?' Scarlett asked.

'Cudgel,' Cudgel said after having a little think.

'And what is it that you really want? If you could wish for anything – anything in the world?'

'To eat you three,' Cudgel said, not having to think at all about that question.

'Right, this isn't going to plan. Okay, who's the biggest giant in these plains?'

'Bludgeon, then his sister, then me. We're the five biggest giants in the plains.'

'And the smartest too, I bet.'

'Yep. Bludgeon is the smartest of us giants. He's always having good ideas. Like the time he drew an arrow on a piece of paper pointing to his crater because he kept getting lost.'

'Yes, that is very clever,' Scarlett said, confused.

'Even better than that. Because he kept losing the bit of paper too, he got the arrow pointing to his home tattooed on his face instead. Only, he couldn't see it. So, he got the arrow tattooed on his arm instead. That way he couldn't lose it and he could see it and he would always know which way home was.'

'Right. Great idea,' Scarlett said, slowly shaking her head, eyes wide.

'It was until his sister pulled his arm off. She was jealous cos she was always getting lost too.'

'Geniuses, both of them!'

'Yeah, Bludgeon gets all the best food and still gets to sleep the most.'

'So, how would you like to be even smarter than him?' Scarlett asked.

'How?'

'Tilia here knows a potion for that.'

'I do?' Tilia asked, pointing to herself.

'She does. It's very similar to the potion for earache, isn't it?' Scarlett said, giving Tilia a little kick, her eyebrows raised.

'Nope. The potions are very, very different,' Tilia said, shaking her head.

Cudgel looked back to Scarlett with a frown.

'Different in their effect, she means. But the ingredients are identical,' Scarlett said, and gave Tilia another friendly kick to the shin.

'Owww!' Tilia yelped and went to say something else, but Scarlett kept going.

'We should start getting the ingredients ready.'

'But I want it now!' Cudgel shouted.

'It's going to take us at least two hours to get your potion ready,' Scarlett said, with an apologetic shrug.

'Too long. You only have three hours!' Cudgel bellowed, holding up four, massive fingers.

'Understood. Right, Tilia, what ingredients went into the potion that helped the villagers of Hapglade take their minds off their earaches?'

'Oh, right! I understand now,' Tilia said with a wink. 'First, we'll need cornswood herb, and tangle-weed – a good basket full. Then we'll need a bowl of dinkle berries ... ' and Tilia listed about twenty shrubs and weeds they had to find for the potion. Cudgel knew a few of these plants by name and others by description. They stuck together and began their search where the giant told them to look.

'You've managed to do it again,' Blondie whispered over to her.

'What do you mean?'

'You've managed to talk us out of being eaten – again! I admire you, Scarlett. I don't always like your stealing and tricking, but it saved my life a few times now. So, I guess I just wanted to say I'm sorry.'

'Hey, no problem. To be honest, I just work on instinct,' Scarlett said, shrugging.

'I wish I could. I think I can remember making a list about

what lists I needed to make that day,' Blondie smiled back.

'I'm glad you're not still mad at me about wandering off to find the coins.'

Their hunt for all the herbs and weeds and berries wasn't made any easier, though, by the fact the giant was always next to them, peering over their shoulders and generally staying close in case they decided to run.

Running would have been a bad idea, though, Scarlett concluded, although the thought crossed her mind again a few times. The plains were flat with barely a bush to hide behind for miles and, as stupid as the giant was, his legs were at least four times as long as hers. Even if she could distract him and sprint off, he'd soon catch up and then she doubted she would get a chance to talk her way out of it a second time.

Just before their allotted three hours had expired, they had collected all the ingredients that Tilia needed. Cudgel took them back to his hole, which was really just a deep rut in the ground where he slept, and Tilia began heating a giant cauldron of ditch water over a fire. She climbed into the barrel of herbs and weeds to tread them down and then climbed out and added them to the cauldron as she began to sing:

> We met a giant who was a meanie,
> And Scarlett told him I was a genie,
> And he believed it cos his brain was teeny,
> Giants are so thick!
> He didn't know how to use his wish,
> so now we're cooking up a dish,
> that smells a little bit like fish,
> Giants aren't very bright!

He'll drink it down cos he's a dummy,
And probably think it's very yummy,
But it's gonna explode in his tummy,
Giants are so thick!'

This was all sung very loudly with Cudgel sitting just a few feet away from Tilia as she worked.

'That song!' Cudgel said, rising to his feet, towering over them all, a frown growing across his forehead, making his monobrow dip in the middle. 'It's pretty. Although, I prefer songs that rhyme.'

Tilia ignored him and leant over the cauldron taking a few good sniffs. 'That's about done I reckon. Right, Cudgel, you must drink the whole thing down.'

Smiling, the giant lifted the huge cauldron as if it were a thimble and quaffed the potion down in one gulp, tossing it aside afterwards. What followed was the loudest burp, maybe even the loudest sound, that Scarlett had ever heard.

'Am I smart now?' the giant asked.

'It takes a few moments. Just wait a minute,' Scarlett reassured him.

The giant looked around for a bit and scratched his head. Then his hand absentmindedly (although Scarlett was quite sure that Cudgel did most things absentmindedly) began to stroke his tummy.

'My belly don't feel too good,' Cudgel said with a moan.

'Right, get ready!' Scarlett whispered.

'My belly don't feel too good at all. It's gone all dizzy and bubbly.'

'Right, run for it!' Scarlett shouted as she took Cudgel's belly making the strangest gurgling sounds as their signal to leave as fast as they could.

12

The Questionable Sir Fox

SCARLETT LED THE CHARGE, TEARING OFF away from the giant who made one staggering movement to give chase then pulled up abruptly, doubling over and clutching his middle. As they fled towards Bitterfall, the most disturbing noises came from the giant behind them. Only once did Scarlett risk a glance back to see if they were being pursued. Cudgel was on his hands and knees and wasn't at all interested or capable of getting up and giving chase. She kept up the pace until her legs cramped and her sides felt as though they would burst.

They must have run a good mile and a half at almost top speed when Scarlett collapsed, sucking in deep, desperate breaths. It took her a few moments to get the strength back to even start walking again. It was only when a most unpleasant smell drifted downwind from the direction of the giant, accompanied by deep, angry shouts, that Scarlett pushed herself to a jog. By this time, though, they could clearly see the stone buildings of Bitterfall, with Crimsin's castle looming over them, like a dark, stone giant dwarfing the little two-story thatched buildings of the town.

'Wow! That stinks,' Blondie said as they slowed their pace, reaching the first of Bitterfall's houses. 'How can a smell be that bad? Tilia, you are one mean cook!'

Where Bitterfall had looked an inviting refuge just moments before, now, in the shadow of the mountain-like castle, it was dark and foreboding. The white paint on the walls was dull and peeling. Windows were boarded up and the cobblestones were covered in grime. Few plants grew in the absence of the sun. Only yellowing nettles and weeds managed to survive. The animals that moved about on two legs skulked around and kept close to the buildings, moving stealthily with their faces covered by their dark clothes. A family of skinny mice, soot-covered and forlorn, scuttled past, their faces long and low. A badger with a wooden leg sat on the steps of a crumbling house just staring at his dirty, bandaged paws.

'Let's find The Cruel Crow Inn quickly and keep a low profile,' Scarlett said, pulling up her hood. Keeping in the shadows, she led the way, avoiding eye contact with the thin, haunted animals that passed her by, her gaze kept to the weed-covered road. She only risked glancing up to look at the names of buildings. Suddenly, a grey squirrel dressed in olive and brown rags, turned tail and ran, nearly knocking Scarlett over. Other creatures scurried away too into crumbling houses and back alleys. Some deep, animal instinct kicked in, and she grabbed Tilia and Blondie and pulled them around the side of a house. Just then, a deep, throaty growl grew close, as did the scraping sound of claws on the cobblestones. Scarlett pressed herself against the wall and tried to make herself as insignificant as possible. The sound started to move away, and she saw the back of a two-legged wolf leading a real wolf on a chain. The bipedal wolf was dressed in clothes similar to those that the Beefeaters of the Tower of London wear: deep reds and black and gold.

'Quick, let's keep going,' Scarlett said, taking Blondie by the hand and heading off down the road, making their way ever closer to Crimsin's castle. Twice more they saw wolf guards patrolling the streets, but they kept their distance and only crossed the roads when it was all clear. By now, they were quite lost. The town had only looked small from the other side of the plains and beneath the behemoth of a fortress that stood over it, but the roads kept going with more and more alleys and backstreets and small lanes leading off in all directions.

As twilight settled in Scarlett had reached the far side of Bitterfall and she could see a narrow stretch of land between the town and the bridge that led to the castle. In front of the bridge, wolves roamed and passed backwards and forwards. There were other creatures there too – big, black birds in robes and fat rodents in leather armour. She would deal with them later. For now, she needed to find this Sir Fox behind The Cruel Crow Inn.

Scarlett had seen The Rotten Rat Pub, The Fat Monkey Tavern, The Lazy Dragon Boarding House and it wasn't until she had almost given up hope at the last few buildings in Bitterfall, when she found The Cruel Crow Inn. It was a white, two-storey stone building, with a sign that creaked in the breeze. The wind seemed to be different here, like the cold that sweeps in before a storm. A crow with a gold coin in its mouth was painted on the inn's sign and the sounds of harsh laughter and raised voices could be heard from behind its dark windows.

From their position in the shadows between two empty houses, they watched The Cruel Crow Inn and its unsavoury patrons. A rat as tall as Scarlett crept in and then left a few minutes later with a small bundle. Some other unpleasant looking creatures came and went, but no wolf guards.

'We should wait outside!' Blondie said, looking up and down the dirt lane.

Scarlett frowned at her. 'I'm not freezing to death out here. Not with all the wolf guards we've seen around. Plus, I'm hungry and tired. We'll all wait inside and see if we can get something to eat. It can't be more dangerous than out here', and, taking a deep breath, Scarlett walked over to the inn and pushed the door open.

The inn fell silent and every sharp-featured face and beady eye turned to her. A gang of human-sized magpies sat around a small table to her right playing cards, their eyes black and unreadable. One giant, angry looking bull with an eye patch sat alone in the corner staring at her over a barrel-sized tankard of frothy beer which he held in one hoof. On her left, two weasels whispered to each other and then gave Scarlett wide smiles. The bartender, a big ram with a badly stitched scar on his face, was wiping a glass with a rag that looked as though it had just been dug up.

'This looks nice,' Tilia said, pushing forwards and walking over to a stool at the bar. 'Do you do cappuccinos?' she asked the bartender, who glared at her for a moment and then disappeared into a room behind the counter.

Scarlett walked over to Tilia, conscious all eyes were still on her, and gave Tilia's sleeve a tug. 'Blondie was right, let's wait outside!'

Just then the bartender reappeared with a mug and saucer and placed it down on the counter. 'Sprinkles?' he asked, gruffly.

'Oooh! Yes, please,' Tilia said, clapping her hands together as the bartender shook the container over Tilia's coffee with a swift flick of the wrist leaving a perfect flower pattern of cocoa on the top. 'What's wrong?' Tilia asked as she blew on her coffee.

'This place doesn't look safe,' Scarlett said, confused by the cappuccino but still not warming to the place. Following Tilia, who took her coffee over to a table next to where the two weasels were now arguing, she took up a seat where she was best hidden. The weasels next to them were getting heated. Their debate had quickly escalated into pushing with lots of pointing of claws and snarling.

Tilia looked around her, at the angry bull with the eyepatch, at the fighting weasels, then back to Scarlett.

'Not safe? You think the cups might be dirty?'

'No, Tilia. I think we'll end up in a fight here!'

Tilia looked around her again, disbelieving. 'What? In here?'

'Yes, Tilia, look around you – at that ugly bull, the fighting weasels and the cardplaying magpies.'

'Nonsense. They're just regular folk like you and me,' Tilia said, but could obviously tell that Scarlett didn't believe her. 'Look, I'll show you', and she leant over to the two weasels that were now squaring off against each other. 'What are you two talking about?'

'This idiot here thinks that the clotted cream goes on the scone first!' the taller weasel said.

'And this buffoon here thinks that the jam should go first!' the smaller weasel replied.

'Well, that's nonsense,' said Tilia, smiling, and they both looked at her, unsure whose side she was taking. 'The butter goes first!'

The two weasels looked at each other for a moment and then burst out laughing, which started Tilia laughing and soon the three of them were all supporting each other as they fell about.

Scarlett rolled her eyes and felt brave enough to go over to the bar and order herself a glass of water. The water came out in a chipped and cracked porcelain mug and looked the colour of bath water after a long soak. After taking a few sips, Scarlett decided that bath water would probably have been preferable. When she returned to the table, Tilia was telling the weasels, and the bull who had joined them, about how Scarlett had thought that fairies could fly, which everyone thought was just about the funniest thing they had ever heard.

'Yes, thank you, Tilia,' Scarlett said, sarcastically. The bull was slapping his thigh and calling over to the magpies to come and hear how stupid Scarlett was. Scarlett didn't mind, though; she would prefer to be laughed at than eaten.

The bartender brought over some food for everyone, paid for by the bull who said he hadn't heard anything so funny in years, and neither Blondie, Tilia nor Scarlett refused. Scarlett and

Blondie kept a low profile, happy to eat their bread and hard cheese at the edge of the circle of creatures, with Tilia in the middle. Only when the magpies insisted on playing cards with them did Scarlett really speak much at all. It took a few rounds for Scarlett to learn the rules as the game was new to her. It involved collecting certain cards and passing others on to hinder your opponents. She soon saw how to cheat and take extra cards and save others under her leg for later. The magpies were cheating too, of course, and only Blondie seemed to be playing properly and losing badly as a result. Playing cards and cheating, Scarlett soon forgot her troubles and started whistling, as she often did when she was feeling carefree. She won a milk bottle top, a safety pin and a small, shiny spoon which the magpies seemed to covet greatly. The magpies were excited by anything shiny and so Scarlett was happy to lose a coin that she had found in the Luz Mala Marshes to them.

Their night was brought short, though, when, from somewhere on the far side of town, they heard the bells striking midnight.

'Tilia, we should be going,' Scarlett said to the other two, who agreed.

They said their goodbyes, thanked the animals and barman for a lovely evening, and left.

'Come on, let's get this done quickly,' Scarlett said, walking around to the back of The Cruel Crow Inn. She stopped and her heart sank. There was no one there. Then, just as she was about to suggest going back inside, there was a red glow from the end of a pipe and two orange eyes lit up, the dark, oval pupils alert and dangerous. A fox, dressed in dark brown tweeds, stepped out of the shadows, blowing rings of smoke as the moonlight revealed him.

'Scarlett, I presume?' Sir Fox said in a gravelly, but well-spoken, voice.

'How do you know who I am?' Scarlett asked, shocked. She had hoped that she would be unknown to him and that by knowing *his* name and reputation, it might give her some advantage. That was clearly not going to be the case now.

'It's my business to know who everyone is, what they want and how much they can afford to pay,' Sir Fox said with a sly grin.

'I have barely anything to pay, I'm afraid. Not even my shadow,' Scarlett apologised, turning the pockets of her red puffer jacket inside out.

'I've heard you have a pretty nice mirror on you,' Sir Fox said, putting the pipe back into his mouth and blowing another ring of blueish smoke.

'Then your information is out of date, I'm afraid. Rancan has the mirror in exchange for our release.'

'That's too bad, then. I doubt you have anything else to offer,' Sir Fox said, as he slowly stepped back into the shadows.

Scarlett took out the iron coin from her pocket and showed it to Sir Fox. His eyes sparkled in the moonlight for a second and then faded. 'Maybe if it was real gold. You found that in the Luz Mala Marshes, didn't you? Fool's gold, and I'm no fool.'

'Wait, there must be something I can trade. How about my jacket?' she said, starting to take it off.

'What would I want that ghastly thing for? No, I'm afraid you're out of luck. Come back when you have something to exchange.'

'Hey, I don't even know what I'm getting for my money!' Scarlett said, getting angry. She wasn't going to come all this way to be denied now.

'As you may have seen behind you, there is a bridge to Crimsin's castle some way off, which is guarded by a pack of wolves. The wolves are all watched by the rats who are watched by the crows that circle up high. There are wards and spells stopping anyone from getting onto the bridge. Forget her army of vermin, those spells are the toughest part to get past. But I can do it for you. For a price.'

'I know a spell that can get us through that!' Tilia said, and everyone ignored her.

'Now I *do* know how to make an enchantment that can get you across the bridge, and, with the help of your companions, I can distract the guards long enough for you to get across. But I'm risking my neck here. It's not going to be cheap,' Sir Fox said, tapping out the tobacco from his pipe and tucking it away in one of his many pockets.

'Fine, then let's make a deal,' Scarlett said, holding out her hand. 'If you can get me across that bridge and I come out alive with my shadow, you can have all the gold I can carry out with me.'

Sir Fox laughed. 'You honestly believe you're coming out of there?'

Scarlett nodded. 'I do.'

'Good for you,' Sir Fox smiled. 'However, I'm a betting man, and that's a pretty lousy bet. Chances are you'll be dead or in chains within the first few minutes of getting inside and then I'll have done all that hard work for nothing.'

'You can have my whistle. I've always been told I have a good whistle,' Scarlett said and whistled the first few bars of the *Scooby Doo* theme tune. 'You can take it now until I return,' Scarlett said, crossing her arms as if this were a take it or leave it offer. 'It's insurance. If I come out, I get my whistle and you get the gold. If I don't, you keep my whistle.'

'Interesting,' Sir Fox said, and moved his paw in front of Scarlett's mouth, as if taking away a loose hair or cobweb. She felt a breath of air escape her lips unbidden and heard a little sigh that must have come from her. Sir Fox put the paw to his own lips and began to whistle. It was Scarlett's whistle coming out of his mouth. Scarlett pursed her lips and tried to whistle herself again, but nothing came out.

'Then we have a deal?' Scarlett asked, trying not to panic that she had now lost her whistle and her shadow.

'It just so happens I have some friends that pay a lot for a person's whistle. It's a deal then. But, there's just one final, little test that you need to take before we start', and he rummaged around in a hessian sack and took out two large mushrooms. One was bright red and looked like the colour of a ripe pepper, the other was black and withered with grey stripes. 'You must take a bite of one of these mushrooms. One will make you sleep for a very long time. Hundred years, possibly. The other is harmless and eating it is the first part of the spell I need to cast.

The trouble is, I can't help you choose,' Sir Fox said matter-of-factly. Scarlett glared at him for a while then at the mushrooms he held in either paw. She didn't have the first idea how magic worked, but she didn't want to get tricked. There was something in his cold, orange eyes, though, that made her feel this wasn't a trap and that it was part of some enchantment that she needed to pass.

Her hand hovered over the red mushroom, before picking up the black one. Worried she would wimp out, she, without hesitating any longer, took a bite and placed it back into his paw. A not-unpleasant liquorice taste filled her mouth. She waited for some ill effect to kick in, sleepiness or cramps or blindness or shrinking, but nothing happened.

Sir Fox grinned. 'How did you know which one to take?'

Scarlett shrugged. 'Well, I've learnt that things are never what they seem in Knoware. For instance, Crimsin looked like a weak old lady and the coins I found in the marshes looked golden, but they're not what they looked like. Then there are other things that look dangerous, like The Cruel Crow Inn and Mummy Bear, but they're actually nice. That's what I was hoping for with the mushroom.'

'Well done. Then that is the first part of the enchantment. The second part of what is needed will take a few moments to make. You'll need to bring me back seven daisies. Keep the stems long. You shouldn't have trouble finding them, even in Bitterfall. It's important that you pick them yourself, not your friends, although they can help you find them.'

Scarlett was too tired and too close to the end to question Sir

Fox or magic in general, so she began searching around for the flowers whilst Blondie and Tilia waited with Sir Fox. They all agreed that they would look pretty stupid if they all went off looking for daisies and came back to find that Sir Fox was long gone with Scarlett's whistle. It didn't take Scarlett many minutes, though, to find a small patch of a dozen or so daisies growing on a piece of scrub land. She picked seven daisies and took them back to where Sir Fox was waiting.

'Good,' Sir Fox said as he nudged them with his paw. 'Now, you need to make a daisy chain. I assume you know how?' Scarlett nodded. 'But as you link each one, you must think of one thing from home that you miss. Just one thing for each of the daisies as you link them. You must picture that thing clearly in your mind. Understand?'

Nodding her understanding again, Scarlett sat down on one of the crates at the back of the inn and, in the moonlight, picked up one of the daisies. As she pressed her nail through the stem, she thought of her mum. She threaded the next daisy through the hole and then pressed another small cut and thought of her dad waiting at the station. Then her dog – and she quickly stopped. She didn't have a dog. It was getting harder and harder to picture home. Her gran, she could still picture her gran thanks to Oma so that was number three. She tried to picture her room and managed to visualise most of it, but nothing she'd really miss. But then she focused on home and remembered she had two homes. So, she pictured both buildings for the fourth and fifth daisies. With her palms on her temples, eyes squinted, she tried to remember her friends. Lily came to mind first; she had a feeling she was one of her best friends, so she was number six. Poppy ... she pictured a girl called Poppy and remembered that she was good friends with her too, so Poppy was the final daisy to complete the chain. 'Finished!' she proudly proclaimed.

'Good, now put it over your head. It will tie you to your world, a bit like your shadow did. It will make you invisible to spells, as long as you hold your breath as you go under the first archway. After that, you can breathe. The bridge is longer than it looks. I don't want you dying before you even get to the castle because you tried to hold your breath the whole way,' Sir Fox said, helping her slip the floral necklace over her head. 'Now, just in case you do get caught by Crimsin, it would be a huge boon to my life expectancy if you weren't wearing this necklace. See, it wouldn't take Crimsin long to work out who had helped you make it and then I'd have a small army after me,' Sir Fox said.

'You want me to take it off before I go in?'

'If it wouldn't be too much trouble,' Sir Fox grinned.

'Fine. So, what are you going to do about those guards?'

13

Crimsin

SIR FOX HAD GONE OVER THE plan three times, once for Scarlett and Blondie, then twice more for Tilia.

'So, when do I jump out of the cake?' Tilia asked after a moment's reflection.

'There is no cake, Tilia. You were the one that mentioned the cake!' Scarlett said, waving her hands in annoyance.

'Okay, okay. Got it,' Tilia said apologetically.

'Tell me it back then,' Scarlett ordered, not at all convinced she had got it.

'So, Blondie and I will cause a fuss and then run off between the houses over there. Sir Fox will raise a tripwire to cause confusion and give us time to escape. We run into The Cruel Crow Inn and make ourselves scarce,' Tilia said, listing the parts off on her fingers.

'Yes!' Scarlett said, surprised.

'No cake?' Tilia timidly asked.

'No cake,' Scarlett reassured her.

The four of them nodded to each other.

'Good luck, Scarlett,' Blondie said, and hugged her. It was so unexpected, that it took Scarlett a few seconds to react, but she recovered quickly enough to hug her back.

'Good luck to you too. And you, Tilia!' Scarlett said, taking a deep breath. 'I'll have our shadows and your scissors back before you know it.'

Tilia tapped the side of her head with her finger. 'Don't worry about me. I've got a spell ready just in case.'

'Well, that's a relief,' Scarlett smiled. 'Right, let's go!'

After checking her daisy chain was still on, she went and got in position. She crouched a little further away, where the town ended and a flat stretch of land before the castle began. Scarlett nodded across the street to where Blondie and Tilia were hiding.

Tilia and Blondie stepped out of the shadows behind The Cruel Crow Inn and began to shout and holler as loud as they could, jumping up and down and waving their arms.

'They've seen us, they're coming over!' Tilia squealed excitedly as Scarlett saw a mob of wolves and rats begin to run over to them.

'I know, let's get going!' Blondie shouted and dragged Tilia off between the houses.

For the moment then, the bridge was unguarded, but Scarlett knew it wouldn't be like that for long. As the crows began to wheel away from the bridge and towards the town, she ran for it. The ground was rough and uneven, but she made it to the bridge without anyone or anything seeing her.

In front of her stretched the bridge over the moat to Crimsin's castle. It was a wooden bridge, wide enough for two people to walk side-by-side together. Although it was made of worn, neat timbers, the railings were rounded wooden poles painted in terracotta, the same colour as the archway that rose in front of her. The arch was made of two thick wooden poles with a third laid across the top like something from Stonehenge. Checking her daisy chain again, she took a deep breath, held it and began to walk.

The bridge had only looked forty or so yards across, but Scarlett found she had been walking for a long while now and, if anything, the castle seemed further off then when she had started. She exhaled and began to pant after holding her breath for so long. She was sure she must be safe by now. Turning back, she imagined the bridge to be like the train tunnel back in Hapglade, where she would walk and walk and never get any further, but the start of the bridge was so far back now that it was completely out of sight. Behind her there was nothing but the bridge stretching across an ocean into the distance in a perfectly straight line.

When she turned forward again, the castle was way off, a tiny speck at the other end of the bridge. Curdled pink and orange clouds blanketed the sky above her from horizon to horizon, as if the sun were setting all around and not just in the west. She walked to the edge of the bridge and climbed onto the first rung to peer over the edge. The clouds weren't reflected in the blue of the sea which gently bobbed and plopped against the supporting pillars. It was as if the sea reflected a different sky altogether. She carefully stepped back onto the bridge, her head swaying a little from the drop.

Putting her hands into the pockets of her red puffer jacket, her hood pulled up, she carried on across the bridge. It was a long walk and she recapped everything that had happened since she had woken up in the three bears' house what seemed like a lifetime ago. She tried to remember what her life had been like before she came to Knoware and then the castle seemed to be right in front of her. Looking back, she could see that the other side of the bridge where she had paused before the archway was just a good stone's throw away.

Now she stood in front of massive double doors that she couldn't have touched the top of if she had been the size of Cudgel. Scarlett suddenly felt very small and ill-prepared. The doors were made of red steel, with rivets the size of her fist and she doubted whether the troll could have even smashed through them. She looked for an alternative route in. The bridge came flush up to the castle doors with a drop either side. She didn't even contemplate climbing the walls; one, because she was awful at climbing, and two, these walls had no cracks or vines or anything that would have given her a good hand or foot hold. Geckos might have even struggled to scale the wall. What choice did she have but to knock? So, she did. Three hard knocks, except her hard knocks made almost no sound at all on the iron doors. She wasn't even sure that she heard it herself, but a deep booming, clanging sound came from inside the castle to tell her that something was listening.

Scarlett took a step back and, with a creak and a groan, the giant doors began to open outwards. Inside, Scarlett could see a long corridor with stairs at the end that led up.

Well, I've got this far, she thought, and stepped inside. As she did, two torches on either side of her burst into flame. With a gulp, she carried on down the corridor, torches flaring into life as she passed them. Behind her, as she somehow knew they would, the giant doors creaked shut with a definite finality. A boom echoed down the corridor making the torches flicker and stutter.

Scarlett reached the bottom of the stairs and looked up. There was no going back now, even if she wanted to.

'One, two, three ... ' she counted the steps as she climbed. She didn't know why, but she needed to do something. ' ... thirteen, fourteen, fifteen ... ' she muttered as she got halfway, a cold draft floating down. Above her, Scarlett could see the high ceiling of a hall, midnight blue with faded gold symbols. ' ... twenty-four, twenty-five ... ' Scarlett counted as more of the room above came into view. It was a cavernous hall, with stone pillars at the sides that curved into arches above.

'Twenty-seven,' she said as she stepped into the hall. Despite the long, thin windows on either side of the cathedral-like chamber, the room was gloomy, and Scarlett saw that it was night outside. Wind and rain lashed against the panes, even though it had been perfectly sunny just a few moments ago outside.

In front of her, some fifty paces away, was a throne. It was a giant chair that seemed to be made of twisted stone roots, more natural than man-made – or perhaps unnatural would have been a more fitting word. Dark tendrils of stone rose from the floor, like the roots of some hideous tree that was petrified as it was halfway through tearing itself free of the earth. The stone vines twisted and overlapped to form the empty chair and then climbed up into a bough that supported a huge, glass sphere the size of an elephant. Inside the glass sphere, black clouds of mist seemed to writhe and float about. Then Scarlett noticed what it was that was truly swimming and twisting around inside the globe. Shadows! Dozens of shadows! Black, ghostly forms of children trapped within. Ghosts, souls, shadows, darkened reflections writhed over and over each other.

The horror of what Crimsin had done to her, to so many, sank in. She had stolen so much, so many. And then, with sickening horror, she recognised her own shadow, fists banging on the glass, its hood up as it was when it was cut away from her on the bridge. Scarlett clutched at her stomach. It felt like her insides had been pulled out and a gaping hole, where her soul once was, remained. She didn't notice, but she must have fallen because she found herself kneeling, hot tears running down her face.

Then, cutting through her sobs, she heard laughter coming from behind her. Cold, hollow laughter. A door at the back of the hall, behind the stairs she had just climbed, opened and there was Crimsin. No longer old and weathered, Crimsin was tall, elegant and graceful. Not like a ballet dancer is graceful, Scarlett thought, but how a panther is graceful and beautiful and elegant, just before it decides to rip your throat out. Her hair was a dark black but scattered with bright purple flowers. Her skin was grey, like polished marble and she wore a dress that seemed to be woven from brambles. She regarded Scarlett with a thorny stare from her green eyes.

Flanking Crimsin were two crows, each six-foot tall and dressed in red military jackets and tall hats. They held large pikes and walked alongside Crimsin, their eyes blank and emotionless, scattering petals and flower heads in front of her as she walked.

'I was going to ask you how you got in here, but I can see someone has made you a little charm,' Crimsin said, approaching Scarlett and admiring the daisy chain around Scarlett's neck. Crimsin's voice was high and rich and elegant, but with a deep bass behind it, as if it were being played through huge speakers. Crimsin glided above Scarlett where she was still flopped on the floor. Her footsteps, if her feet were even touching the floor, were silent – or at least hidden beneath the scratchy steps of her crow guards, sharp talons scraping against stone. Reaching out, Crimsin ripped the daisy chain from Scarlett's throat but then dropped it as if it had bitten her. 'Powerful. Very powerful. Who made it?' Crimsin spat, her smile gone.

Scarlett's heart sank. She had promised Sir Fox. He had kept his word and she had let him down. She stayed silent and stared at the floor. Years of practice in detention with Ms Pridham, being grilled over who had helped Scarlett draw moustaches on the poster of the kings and queens of England, or who had stolen all the compasses in maths, had taught her to stay tight lipped.

'Not talking? Fine. Oma? No, not this far north,' Crimsin said, pacing up and down but never taking her eyes from Scarlett. 'The owls maybe? No, I doubt they would be so bold. Sir Fox then? Yes, of course. Sir Fox!' Crimsin said with a grin. 'Guards!' she yelled out, and from the darkness of a corridor to one side came striding a grey wolf, walking on his hind legs and dressed in battered silver armour. Behind him was an old raven with patches of white feathers and milky eyes who was dressed in purple robes. 'Go and find our old friend, Sir Fox. Dead, if needs be! He has overstepped the mark this time.'

The wolf and raven bowed deeply and turned away, not noticing or caring that Scarlett was even there.

'What did you hope to achieve by coming here?' Crimsin said after a moment's thought, turning back to her.

Scarlett could feel her jaw moving but no words came out. 'I want my shadow back,' she finally managed to stammer, hoping that somewhere out there, Sir Fox was hiding or leaving Bitterfall far behind him.

Crimsin smiled, like a mother might smile at a child's ridiculous request. 'No. Your shadow's mine now. I really should have nipped all this nonsense in the bud back in the forest when I had the chance. My wolves were so close. If Oma's shadow had not got in my way, it would have all been over. Never mind. I have you now.'

'Why? Why did you take my shadow?' Scarlett asked, looking for some kind of weakness.

'The shadows give me power, of course. They give me immortality and beauty and youth and strength. I slowly draw from the magic they contain. And, quite frankly, I will make better use of it than you will. They help me stay loved and feared by everyone in the whole of Knoware,' she grinned, and showed her sharp, pointed teeth.

'You're horrible and shallow,' Scarlett spat back.

'Please. Wanting to be adored and feared isn't shallow. It is the deepest, most primal desire we have. You might want to be adored or feared for your mind, or your creativity or your beauty or strength, but we all want it. It is at the heart of almost every dream anyone has ever had,' she said as she reached behind her and took out the ornate scissors from a belt of brambles around her waist. 'These scissors can cut through anything. Shadows, reflections, dreams, and now you can live in the castle with me, slowly aging whilst you watch me become more powerful and more beautiful,' Crimsin said, and admired the scissors as the flashes of lightning outside caught the detailed patterns carved into the handles. Then, after slipping them back into her belt, she looked to the guards at her side. 'Take her to the dungeons!'

Taking her roughly by the arms, the crow guards began to lead her away. At first, Scarlett acted as if she fully intended to be led away without protest, then, as the guards' grip loosened, she shook them off and darted at Crimsin, wrapping her arms around her waist as she slammed into her like a rugby player. Crimsin staggered back, Scarlett holding on tightly, but despite the impact, she never fell. Scarlett let go, her head dropping, embarrassed, her hands disappearing inside the sleeves of her jacket like a tortoise's head retreating into the safety of its shell.

Crimsin slapped her hard around the face with the back of her hand. Time stood still for a moment. Having been unable to raise her hands in time, the blow had numbed Scarlett's senses. It seemed as though the sound had suddenly been turned down because she could see Crimsin's lips moving but couldn't hear what she said. All she could focus on was the ringing in her ears, and the burning of her cheek. With her left hand, she dabbed at her swollen lip and felt blood. A coppery, metallic taste filled her mouth as the guards grabbed her again and took her off, this time not allowing their grip to relax. Despite the fiery feeling on her cheek and the split lip, Scarlett smiled as the crow guards took her away. She would soon be getting her shadow back!

14

The Dungeon

HER CORVID JAILERS LED HER AWAY through a side exit of the main hall and then down a long corridor. As she descended down several flights of winding stairs, the walls became darker, damper and the smell of mould and dust grew thicker, as if this part of the castle had died many thousands of years ago. After ripping her backpack from her, they tossed Scarlett into a small stone cell where the momentum sent her sprawling into the corner. They slammed an iron gate shut behind her and locked it with a large, rusty key. Cawing loudly to each other, the two guards left and paid her no more attention, tossing her backpack into the corner and hopping back off up the stairs.

It took a few moments for the ringing in her ears to stop before Scarlett stood up and walked over to the bars to see where she was. It was a long corridor of jail cells.

'Well, we're back in prison again,' Blondie's voice came from the cell opposite.

'Hey, you guys are here!' Scarlett said with genuine excitement, making Blondie out in the dark now.

'I distracted them for as long as I could, Scarlett. I was just about to cast a confusion spell, but the wolves grabbed me,' Tilia apologised, looking down to the floor.

'That's okay, Tilia. You did great!' Scarlett beamed.

'I did? Really? Even though I couldn't find the cake?'

'Really you did! And there was no cake, Tilia.'

Blondie huffed. 'Well, a fat lot of good it did us. We distracted them for as long as we could, but the wolves stormed The Cruel Crow and found us. We're all in her dungeon now, without our shadows and with no hope of escape. It's Rancan's cave all over again!'

'We did tell you it was a waste of your time, didn't we?' a familiar voice came from further down the corridor. Scarlett pressed her face against the bars to see Gabrielle with her brother Hayden captive two cells down from Tilia.

'Wow, you guys are here too! That's great,' Scarlett said, almost laughing. 'We can all get our shadows back together.'

Blondie grabbed the bars with both hands, her face red. 'What are you talking about, Scarlett? Are you losing the plot? We're going to die here!'

Scarlett simply smiled back. 'Nope, we're not. I'll explain. But first, I have an apology to make.'

'What is it this time?' Blondie asked, short of patience.

'I stole something,' Scarlett shrugged.

Blondie rolled her eyes. 'Scarlett, this is hardly the time.'

'It's exactly the time,' Scarlett said, her right hand emerging from the sleeve of her jacket holding the ornate scissors. 'Crimsin said they can cut through anything. That true, Tilia?'

'You got them back! You said you would, and you did, you bloomin' marvellous girl! Yes, they will. They'll cut anything!' Tilia said, jumping up and down.

Lining up the blades with the metal bars, it looked as though cutting through them should have been impossible. They were thick iron bars – slightly rusty and very old, but it would still have taken months, maybe even years, of trying to cut through them with a normal pair of scissors. But, just as Scarlett knew they would, the ornate scissors snipped through the bars as if they were made of cheese. With a couple more snips, the gate to her cell fell open with an echoing clang. She strolled over to Blondie's prison next.

'You're really something,' Blondie said nodding, eyes wide.

'Good something? Bad something?'

'Good, I think,' Blondie said with a smile.

With a few quick cuts, Blondie's cage door fell with a clatter. Next, she freed Tilia and the siblings, Hayden and Gabrielle.

'Let's go. We've got shadows to free!' Scarlett said as she picked up her backpack and they all made their way quietly up to the top of the stone stairs, along the corridors and back to the main hall.

'I don't think we're out of the woods yet. Keep your eyes peeled!' Blondie warned, looking all around for danger. 'This all seems too quiet.'

Looking inside the hall from the corridor, Scarlett couldn't see any sign of Crimsin or her guards. Tiptoeing, she edged her way towards Crimsin's throne and the giant, glass orb of shadows. One shadow seemed to be pushing its way in front of the others to lie flat against the glass. It was unmistakably Scarlett's, with its hood up and the clear ridges of the puffer jacket.

'I'm coming, Shadow Me!' she shouted and ran forwards.

Crimsin stepped out from behind the throne, graceful and as carefree as a cat toying with a mouse. Screeching to a standstill, Scarlett almost crashed into her. She instinctively pulled the scissors out and held them in front of her as if she were wielding a dagger.

'And what do you intend to do with them?' Crimsin asked.

Scarlett took a step forward. 'I'm going to break that glass orb and free our shadows. Then I'm going to return the scissors to the lady you stole them from, so I wouldn't get in my way if I were you.'

Crimsin raised her eyebrows in mock confusion. 'But how can you break my shadow vessel and do all that if you cannot even move your arm?'

Scarlett was just about to ask Crimsin what on earth she was talking about when she realised she couldn't move her arm. She couldn't even feel it any longer. It was there, but it felt as if it belonged to someone else, just frozen in place. Her friends behind her were huddled together, helpless and unsure what to do. Crimsin stepped forwards leisurely and without fear.

'In fact, it looks as though your whole body is rooted to the spot,' Crimsin grinned, and Scarlett felt her whole body turning cold and stiff, as if it were iced cement crawling through her veins and not blood. She fell backwards, barely able to move to cushion her fall. The only warmth she felt on her entire body were her hot tears and they rolled down her cheeks and splashed onto the floor.

'Stupid girl. Did you really think you could just walk into my castle and steal my things? I will have to show you what happens to impudent little girls like you,' Crimsin said, and raised her hand as if to strike her.

Scarlett could feel her flesh hardening, as if she were turning to stone and that any strike from Crimsin would shatter her into a thousand pieces. If she could have flinched or raised her hands she would have, but she was frozen and could only watch and cry. As Scarlett realised the end was near, time seemed to slow. Crimsin was above her, fist clenched, ready to strike at the paralysed Scarlett, who was unable to move, or breathe.

But then Crimsin wasn't there anymore. A great beam of light tore above Scarlett's head and struck Crimsin in the chest blasting her across the room as if she had been struck with a cannon ball.

Warmth flooded back into Scarlett's body and she was flesh once more. Her lungs sucked in air in desperate chokes as she tried to work out what had just happened. Where had the beam of light come from? One minute, Crimsin was there, grinning above her, arm raised, then the next a trunk of light had blown her clean across the floor. Scarlett turned around to see what the source was and saw Tilia standing there, the palm of her hand still glowing white.

'I finally managed to get the spell ready!' she said, cheerily, as if the gravity of the situation had not dawned on her.

'You can do magic!' Scarlett stammered.

'Yes,' Tilia said with a smile.

'But really do magic!'

Tilia's smile grew. 'Yes, of course I can. Didn't you believe me?'

Scarlett laughed, but not waiting for Crimsin to get back to her feet, she ran to the shadow orb and struck it with the point of the scissors as hard as she could.

The orb exploded into tiny fragments. Slivers of glass rained down around her, bouncing off her hood. Shadows flew free of their prison like birds fleeing a broken cage. One shadow with a hood and the unmistakable ridges of a puffer jacket flew towards Scarlett and in a flash, which might just have been in her mind or might have been real, she felt her shadow join up to her again. With it came a flood of memories: her mum and dad, her house, her friends, her school – everything.

But then came the laughter. A terrible, high-pitched laugh. Crimsin was getting to her feet, no longer young and graceful and tall. Now she was the old lady that Scarlett had met on the bridge. Thin, wispy and ancient, she was holding something in her gnarled hands. A shadow. Not Scarlett's own shadow – that hid behind her – this was someone else's.

'Ow! That hurts, let go!' Blondie called out from behind Scarlett, her arms wrapped awkwardly around herself, clearly in terrible pain.

'No!' Crimsin smiled, showing her toothless mouth.

'Hey! let her shadow go … ' Scarlett yelled, 'or I'll … '

'Or you will what? You will break my shadow orb? You will release my shadows? You have already played your hand,' Crimsin snarled, twisting the shadow's arm making Blondie fall to her knees and cry out, as if she were bending her real arm.

'Let her shadow go!' Scarlett shouted again, stepping forwards with the scissors held menacingly.

'No. Not until you give me the scissors back!' and Crimsin twisted the shadow's arm further. Blondie screamed out, tears running freely, splashing onto the stone floor.

Running to her side, Scarlett dropped to her knees, putting her arm around her friend. 'Please, stop it.' Scarlett could feel Blondie's sobs and she groaned again. 'You're going to break her arm!'

'The scissors!' Crimsin shouted again, her face screwed into a menacing mess of wrinkles, the shadow helpless in her hands.

'Fine,' Scarlett said, her own tears dripping to the floor next to Blondie's.

'No, Scarlett, just run,' Blondie started, but broke off into another scream of pain. Scarlett, not being able to bear seeing her that way, turned to face Crimsin.

'You want them? Catch!' and Scarlett threw the scissors into the air. Time seemed to slow then as the scissors flashed, whirling towards Crimsin. Down they came towards her in a perfect arc. Then, just as Scarlett was certain they would strike Crimsin, her gnarled hands let go of Blondie's shadow and effortlessly plucked the spinning scissors out of the air, with a cackle of delight.

Blondie's shadow darted away from Crimsin, limping towards Blondie, who rose to meet it. There was a flash of light and they were joined once more. Blondie put one hand up to the side of her head.

'I remember everything!' Blondie said, her eyes wide with amazement.

'Well, don't get used to it. You will all forget everything again soon, my dears. I am taking back my shadows!' and Crimsin began to run towards them, the scissors snipping away in her hand.

Putting her arms around the others, Scarlett turned them towards the entrance and ran. She wasn't sure they could find an exit, but she knew she must try. Sprinting towards the stairs, Scarlett looked back and saw Crimsin, fast for someone who looked so frail, coming towards her. She could see they wouldn't get far, not unless she caused a distraction, not unless she did something.

Scarlett suddenly stopped running and turned on Crimsin like a mouse turning back angrily on the cat that chases it. She knew she couldn't beat Crimsin in a fight, but perhaps she could give her friends enough time to escape. 'No!' Scarlett screamed as she rounded on her, the anger and fear making her voice sound wild. Scarlett's shadow turned with her too, ready to face Crimsin.

Crimsin was so surprised that her prey had turned on her, at the scream, at the anger, at the shadow's lack of fear, that she hesitated for a split second, making her trip. In a blur, Crimsin's leg went flying from under her – made worse by the floor, wet with tears. Crimsin fell forwards heavily, her face screwed up in shock and anger. She came crashing down upon the scissors she was holding, their silver blades disappearing into her chest.

There wasn't even a scream. There was just a soft hissing sound as the pile of black robes sagged and wisps of dust and smoke began to peel away. A roll of thunder outside the castle seemed to abruptly stop and die away. The room brightened.

The others stopped running, halfway down the stairs, and turned to look. They slowly walked back to Scarlett who was still staring at the pile of smouldering rags, half expecting some trick.

'My teacher always said you shouldn't run with scissors,' Scarlett said.

Blondie looked at her and shook her head with a smile. 'Is she dead?'

After a deep breath, Scarlett stepped forward and nudged the rags with her foot. The last of whatever had been Crimsin blew away in coils of smoke. There, gleaming under the rags, though, were the ornate scissors. Bending down, she picked them up and put them into her bag.

'Let's get out of here,' Blondie said.

Scarlett swung her backpack over her shoulder. 'We will. I just have to grab some bits for Sir Fox or else I'm not getting my whistle back.'

It didn't take many minutes of exploring the side rooms and corridors for Scarlett to find what she was looking for. Chests of treasure – diamonds, rubies, sapphires, emeralds, amethysts, all scattered over piles of golden coins. She filled her backpack up with as much as she could carry and went to re-join the others.

'I don't remember there being a huge crack across the floor,' Scarlett said as she met Blondie by the stairs.

'There wasn't. There are cracks appearing everywhere. We need to hurry!' Blondie said, pushing Scarlett towards the exit.

Down in the corridor below, all the lamps were out, and the corridor was in near total darkness. The only light came from a crack in the main doors where the others were struggling to push them open. Scarlett and Blondie joined them, putting their shoulders against the doors and pushing as hard as they could. Unwillingly, the doors creaked open wide enough for them all to squeeze through. They ran across the bridge that began to stretch out in front of them. A cracking noise made Scarlett turn back round and she smiled to see her shadow stop and turn to look too. It felt good to have it back. The noise had come from a giant split that streaked like lighting across the castle's front, mortar and bricks tumbling into the sea below.

'We have to hurry,' Tilia called back. 'We must get off the bridge!'

Scarlett and her shadow ran along the bridge that seemed one moment impossibly long, and Tilia and the others were almost out of sight. The next moment, Scarlett was at the end of the bridge and crashing into them. Panting, they all watched, mesmerised, as Crimsin's castle crumbled away into the sea. Shadows and reflections and ghosts and all sorts of strange shimmering lights and shades seemed to fly from the rubble of Crimsin's castle.

'You did it!' Blondie said, coming over and hugging her. 'You actually did it!'

'*We* did, don't you mean?' Scarlett said. 'I couldn't have done it without you all.'

'So touching,' a silky voice came from behind them and they all turned to see Sir Fox.

'I'm sorry, Sir Fox. I forgot to take the necklace off,' Scarlett said, looking suitably sheepish.

'I know. Every wolf in town was looking for me, but I still know a few holes to hide in.' He eyed Scarlett's weighty bag. 'Can I assume that there are some goodies in there for me?'

Scarlett opened the bag and poured it all out onto the ground. She picked the ornate scissors up, though, and put them back into the bag. 'It's all yours. A deal is a deal, right?'

Sir Fox's orange eyes lit up as he passed his paw over his mouth and then up to Scarlett's lips. 'Your whistle back. A fine whistle to be sure, but this little hoard will do nicely.' Taking a sack out from behind him, Sir Fox began to shovel the treasure into it.

Scarlett held the scissors out to Tilia. 'These belong to you.'

'Thank you, Scarlett,' Tilia said, with tears in her eyes. 'I don't know how to repay you.'

'You've already saved my life. I couldn't have done it without you.' Scarlett watched Tilia admiring the scissors. 'Will it be enough for you to be allowed back into your land?'

'I can't be certain, but I think it will be enough,' Tilia nodded.

'Not tempted to keep a little something?' Blondie asked Scarlett teasingly, looking at the treasure Sir Fox was scraping into the sack.

Scarlett stared at the last of the gems as they sparkled and flashed and then disappeared into the bag. 'No. I'm leaving with a lot more than I came with anyway,' she said, and smiled. 'I guess we should start heading back then. It seems so far to travel, though.'

'It is if you intend to walk back. I'm sure I could talk to the magpies. A few little sparklies from your treasure hoard and they'd be willing to fly you back to Hapglade,' Sir Fox said with a grin.

15

Home

'SCARLETT. I DON'T KNOW HOW TO ever thank you. You've taken back my Lady's Scissors and with these I may hope to be allowed back into the Fay-lands,' Tilia said, a warm smile spreading over her chubby face.

'Tilia. It's me who should be thanking you. You risked your own life to distract the guards and saved my life in the castle. And you can do magic, Tilia. Real magic!'

'Oh, that was just a little bit of child's magic. I'm just pleased it helped.'

'And do you have to return now? Can't you come to Hapglade to see me off?' Scarlett asked, hoping that Tilia would stick with them a little longer.

'Nope. I am going to teleport myself back to the Fay-lands. I shouldn't dally returning the scissors to my queen. I've made that mistake once before.'

Scarlett hugged her and they said more goodbyes. Afterwards, Tilia took three steps backwards and closed her eyes. Her lips began to mumble something – probably an ancient incantation or spell, Scarlett assumed. Then Tilia thrust her hands downwards, her face turning red as she shook at the effort. It was as if electricity were coursing through her body. This shaking and turning ever redder went on for about twenty fairly awkward seconds before Tilia breathed out and relaxed, her face returning to its normal colour.

'As it's a nice day I'm actually going to walk,' Tilia said brightly and turned away off up the road that led further north.

Scarlett watched her for a long time as she walked away, but not once did Tilia look back.

Sir Fox was as good as his word and the magpies agreed to fly Scarlett, Blondie and the two siblings back over the Giant Plains and the Luz Mala Marshes. Scarlett decided not to go directly to Hapglade, but to head to Oma's house first. Being carried by the magpies was made up of brief moments of exhilaration, but it was mainly dominated by the fear of imminent death by falling, being eaten, or torn apart by huge talons. As romantic as the idea of soaring above the trees in the claws of a bird was, Scarlett was incredibly relieved to be placed down on solid ground in a clearing by Oma's house.

Oma was overjoyed to see them all and Scarlett and Blondie enjoyed watching Hayden's and Gabrielle's faces when they first saw Oma and thought it was their own grandmother, and then they were delighted again when watching the siblings see their rooms, exactly how they had remembered them back in their own world and time.

The next morning, after a restful night, they all sat around the table eating toast and drinking tea.

'We'd better get going,' Gabrielle said, standing up with her brother. 'We think we can find the way back from here. Now we have our shadows back, I can feel home almost tugging me. We've spent far too long here. Father will be looking for us.'

They said their goodbyes and Scarlett watched the siblings leave, disappearing off into the forest.

'Well. I guess we'd better get going too,' she said to Oma. 'It's still a few days' journey from here and my dad will be waiting too.'

'Yes, you must. First, I must congratulate you two, though. You are both, despite not getting any older here, blossoming into brave, young women. Knoware will be sad to lose you both. But I'll come with you to see you off,' she said, rising and putting on her coat. Oma led them out of the cottage and, for about an hour, she seemed to do nothing but lead them in large circles around the cottage.

'Are you sure we're going the right way?' Scarlett asked, when she was sure she had passed the same fallen tree for the third time.

'Oh yes,' Oma smiled back. 'The quickest way anywhere is rarely in a straight line', and after passing under a low canopy, the open farm fields of Hapglade suddenly spread out before them.

'We're here!' Scarlett gasped. 'We're back!'

Somewhere between walking and skipping, Scarlett led them through the farm fields to the edge of the village where they raised an uproar as soon as they were spotted. Animals of all kinds came out to greet them as they made their way through the cobbled streets. There was a great commotion and Mummy Bear burst through the crowd and ran to Scarlett, scooping her up and nearly squeezing her to death.

'My little petal. You got your shadow back,' Mummy Bear said, admiring Scarlett's shadow as she put her back down.

'I'm afraid I lost your mirror, though,' Scarlett said, her smile fading.

'That's alright. It was a gift. I hope it was useful. Will you be spending another night here?' Mummy Bear asked hopefully as she walked with Scarlett towards the centre of the village.

'I'm afraid not,' Scarlett apologised.

'And why not?' Daddy Bear suddenly bellowed from behind her, making Scarlett jump a foot in the air.

'The room was lovely, really lovely. I just want to get home and tell everyone how amazing it is!' Scarlett stammered.

Daddy Bear nodded. 'That's fine then.'

Her furry guard of honour led her across the village, then down to the station where the badger ticket inspector was waiting. Here, Scarlett turned to Blondie, who stood beside Oma.

'Blondie, I ... '

'You don't need to say anything,' Blondie said, stepping forwards.

'No, I do. You believed in me and asked for nothing back. You followed me when you didn't have to, and you did it because you thought it was right. I hope that I can take away some of your selflessness,' Scarlett said, a little tear in her eye.

'Well, you've shown me what a real friend is. I don't think I've ever really had one before. And I don't know how you think like you do. You're so clever. I really admire you,' Blondie said, and they both fell into a hug that neither of them wanted to break away from.

'Have we got our shadow back, then?' the badger asked, looking at Scarlett's feet.

'Yes, sir!' Scarlett said, breaking off from Blondie's hug.

'Then you'd better get on board – the train leaves in two minutes,' he said, glancing at his pocket watch then wandering off down the platform.

Scarlett skipped along the platform, excited that she would be seeing her dad in just a few minutes, but as she turned to wave at the train door, she realised she would never be coming back here.

'Will you be alright getting back home?' she shouted to Blondie.

'I think so,' Blondie shouted back over the noise of the bustling crowd that had come to watch. 'Still not sure I'm ready to head back just yet. I might stay at Oma's for a while,' she said, turning to Oma, who smiled back.

'Maybe I'll visit,' Scarlett said, but she knew it was a lie.

The shrill sound of the guard's whistle tore through the noise and Scarlett quickly squeezed on board. Taking a window seat, she waved to everyone. Even the three little pigs had come to see her off.

Suddenly, Blondie broke free of the crowd and ran forward towards the train window. Scarlett stood up. The main window

didn't open, but there was a smaller one above that she managed
to slide upwards.

'What's up?' Scarlett shouted through the gap.

'Take this,' Blondie said, and she took the rose out of her hair
and passed it up. Scarlett squeezed her hand through the window
and took it. They both smiled at each other as another loud toot
of the guard's whistle rang out and the train began to slowly
move along the tracks. Keeping her face pressed against the
window, she watched Blondie waving until the train disappeared
into the tunnel and everything went black.

Scarlett sat back and couldn't decide which emotion was
currently strongest – excitement, confusion, or loss. She couldn't
wait to see her dad again, but she was already missing Blondie,
Oma, Tilia and Hapglade. It was like a dream she'd been woken
up from and wanted desperately to get back into, but was already
fading away.

The relief and exhaustion of the last few days was soon too
much for her, and in the warmth of the dark, she closed her eyes
and slept.

When she awoke, it was to the gentle swaying of the train as it
slowed down. Pressing her face against the window, she could
see Mournt station growing and then there he was – her dad.
She jumped up, waving to him as the train pulled up next to the
platform, Blondie's rose still in her hair.

Her dad waved back, mirroring her big grin, dressed in his
suede jacket and holding out a bunch of red carnations.

'I got you these,' he said, as she jumped down from the train,
'to say sorry that you're missing another party.'

She leapt forwards and wrapped her arms around him and squeezed him so hard that Mummy Bear would have been proud.

'There's nowhere in the world I'd rather be than here,' she grinned.

Thank you for reading *Scarlett in Knoware*.

I hope that you enjoyed reading it half as much as I enjoyed writing it. If you did, please let others know. You can share a link on Facebook, post a photo on Instagram or Snapchat or share an honest review on Goodreads, YouTube or Amazon. You can follow Stuart on Twitter @stuartfryd

Acknowledgements

Thank you to James Hodgson, Peter Randall, Janet Davidson, and everyone at Greenwich Exchange for their unrelenting positivity, faith and hard work. Thank you to Emma Mistry and Nicki Virdee for their amazing work on the cover. Thanks to my beautiful wife, Jayde, who is a constant support and who always believes in me, even when I'm not so sure myself. Danny Boy did an amazing job giving his honest feedback.